TRIGGA

TRIGGA

By

Team Rollock

E-BookTime, LLC
Montgomery, Alabama

TRIGGA

Library of Congress Control Number: 2005939236

ISBN: 1-59824-116-8

First Edition
Published June 2006
E-BookTime, LLC
6598 Pumpkin Road
Montgomery, AL 36108
www.e-booktime.com

Acknowledgements

Team Rollock dedicates this book to Soundview's own Pistol Pete, the man who taught us that his life isn't something that should be emulated but his motivation and drive to get things accomplished is... Much Love! Much Respect!

We are from the streets, therefore we don't drop names. All of our people know who they are so this is how it's going down... We want to thank God, our family, The Rollock's, White's, Dejesus's and Sharpe's for all of their love and support over the years... Without our family this project would have never came to fruition... We also want to thank the entire state of New York for embracing us, and for being proud that we are apart of its history... Love goes out to all of our family members and friends from Roosevelt Island, Mount Vernon, Yonkers and Liver Pool New York... In the Bronx: Soundview Projects, Castle Hill Projects, Webster Projects, Forest Projects, Bronx River Projects, Bronxdale Projects, Throgsneck Projects, Monroe Projects and Patterson Projects... Lafayette, Co-opt City, River Park Towers, Undrecliff Ave, 167th & Clay Ave, 174th Street, Hunts Point, Southern Blvd, University Ave & 183rd Street... In Harlem: Hamilton Place, 145th Street & St Nicholas Ave, 140th Street between 7th & 8th Aves, 117th Street, 116th & Manhattan Ave, 116th Street & Lex, 110th Street & First Ave, Wagner Projects, Jefferson Projects and Foster Projects... In Queens: Woodside Projects, Baisly Projects, Queensbridge Projects, Forty Projects... Lefrak City, Rochdale, Linden Blvd, Guy Brewer and Rockaway Blvds... In Brooklyn: Crown Heights, Marcy Projects,

Acknowledgements

Redhook Projects, Fort Green Projects, Cypress Projects and Coney Island Projects, Lafayette Gardens... The entire Staten Island... We also want to thank all of our family members and friends for their support from Newark New Jersey (Prince Street), Compton California, Portland Oregon, Atlanta, Detroit, Washington D.C., Philly and Baltimore...

Last, but definitely not least, we want to thank all of our true friends in the entertainment industry that have continued to display their undying love and support for us even after the Powers That Be, tried to scare them away... Thank you all for keeping Team Rollock alive...

Falling for You

When you pick me up. If you try to use me like the others, I promise you that your life will never be the same.

The first night we go out, if you hold me right & squeeze me tight, I will happily scream your name.

Sometimes you may want to show me off to get your point across, but never hand me over to your friends.

Trust me, caress me, but don't let just anyone dress with me, because I have made the weakest of boys feel like men.

Normally I am noisy, when I'm getting my grove on, only because that excites people when I'm heard.

Some people when they meet me, they get a little freaky and cover my mouth so they can feel my body speak with silent words.

If you take care of me & oil my body, I will always fulfill your wants & needs.

And I promise if we participate in a threesome, I will bring the third party to its knees.

You must always keep me close, your gonna either love me or love me not, because once you use me & abuse me, if you leave me, you will lose everything you got.

I may seem submissive when ever we interact, but unconsciously I have full control of you.

I talk only when you tell me, but my presence makes you react the way you do hypnotized, that's why you keep me on your side & together we move as one; If you know I would have changed your life this much, I bet you would not have wanted to pick up and use a gun...

In the late 1980's the rate of incarceration of black Americans had ever surpassed that experienced by blacks who still lived under the apartheid regime of South Africa.

This translated into an overrepresentation of fatherless black youth with a confused moral compass and literally no alternative role model to the street legends.

For a variety of reasons, rates of violence including murder, rape and robbery increased dramatically amongst the youth. One's block or projects became lavish as drug profits stayed on the rise.

In any case, whenever creating wealth in the street, security mandates an ability to keep one finger on the pulse of the street and the other on the "trigga".

Contents

Part I

Part II

Part I

"The world is divided between those who live in a dream, believing in right and wrong, good and evil, and those who live with their eyes open, who see there is only power and its prerogatives, reward and punishment…"

Courtesy of Pablo Escobar

The Beginning

January 11, 1988…

It was about 7:30 am in the morning when Tyvon was awaken by the sound of his mothers phone ringing, "Ring! Ring!" He was tired from running the streets the night before so he didn't budge. The phone rang one more time then stopped. Either the person that was calling realized that it was too damn early to be calling somebody's house, or his mom had picked up the phone. Which ever one it was out of the two didn't matter to Ty, he was just glad that the phone stopped ringing so he could go back to sleep. He had been ripping and running for the past three months trying to build up his clientele with the local crack heads and that had him coming in the house later and later every night. He needed his rest not only so he could be of proper competition to the other hustlers on the block, but so he could out run Tinney and the rest of the detectives on the narcotics squad that liked to jump out on him and everybody else that they saw too much.

Just as Ty turned over, trying to get comfortable so he could go back to sleep, he heard his mother calling him from her room.

"Ty!" he ignored her. She waited a second then called again "Tyvon!"

Damn! He said to himself trying to figure out what she could possibly want from him so early in the morning, what ever it was, it must be important. At least in her mind it was. He was hoping that she didn't want him to go to the store or something like that. Finally he worked himself up to answering her. He figured if he answered in his best, I am tired leave me alone whining voice, She would get the picture and let him go back to sleep, "WHUUUTT!"

"Come in here, I have to talk to you." Ty could tell by the sound of her voice that something was wrong. He just couldn't tell how wrong and that was a problem. After taking a deep breath, he rolled out of his bed and walked to his mother's room. As soon as he got to the door he knew what he had sensed was right. His mother was sitting at the edge of her bed and she told him to sit down.

"Ty. Mark, Terrell and Bobby got shot last night in the projects. They're all dead" Her words hit him in the face like a bucket of ice cold water. He didn't want to believe what he was hearing. He was just with Mark and he had saw Terrell on the block right before he came in the house last night and the both of them was just fine. He had never experienced anybody close to him getting killed before so for him to even vision people that he considered his big brothers dead was crazy. Ty felt better thinking and hoping that his mother was misinformed but damn! Who could make up a story like that?

"Ma! I was with them last night and everybody was alright."

"This happened late last night, Ty. Mrs. Watson just called."

Ty sat there stuck, He didn't know what to think but if Bobby's moms had just called, there was nothing more to dispute.

"Are you alright?" asked Ty's mother knowing that he wasn't.

"Yeah, I am good!" said Ty still in shock, "I'm going back to sleep."

Ty walked out the room in silence, He was wondering what could have possibly have happened. Who could have done this? Mark and them were the Big Willies on the block, Nobody fucked with them. Ty knew that he wouldn't be going back to sleep anytime soon. As soon as he washed up and got dressed, he was going to the block to get the scoop.

It seemed like seconds after he left his mothers room her phone was ringing off the hook. The word was spreading quickly and he had to find out what was going on.

After stashing his last two fifty packs of crack in his laundry bag, he quickly got dressed. He threw on his low cut green and white air force ones, some blue Levis jeans, a green champion hoody and his green army jacket. It was time to roll out. He walked out the door and before it closed he heard his mother yelling "keep your ass off that damn corner!"

He was gone.

It was eight in the morning but the whole projects seemed to be outside. Every building Ty walked by had people standing in front talking about what had happened, but since he didn't see anybody from his crew he didn't stop to talk. Just as he passed the building 1715 somebody called him through the broken window on the lobby door, "Yo! Ty." When he turned around he saw his man Jahiem open the door and wave him over.

"What's the word Fam?" Ty said as he entered a hallway full of smoke. Both of his best friends. Kane and Shamel were sitting on the steps smoking a blunt.

"Man! Shit is all fucked up," said Kane, Everybody is buggin out about what happened. You know it's gonna get crazy out here once the team gets together. I already saw Drew walking around strapped the fuck up looking like he's gonna lay somebody down any minute now. It's about to be on out this motherfucker."

"A yo! And you know how Worm and that crazy ass nigga Chris get down. Jahiem added as he passed the blunt back to Shamel. "I haven't seen neither one of them niggas yet, but I know when they come around, there'll be some more fucking bodies dropping tonight."

"Word up," said Shamel taking another pull of the blunt before handing it to Kane.

"Who did it?" asked Ty, staring around at everyone in the lobby waiting for an answer like he was ready to handle things himself.

"People are saying it was Tommy Smalls and them but I don't know," said Kane.

"Yeah! I heard that that motherfucker Tommy was out here a little while ago giving out free bottles to the heads like he was celebrating or something," said Shamel. "Shit! Let El and them put some paper on Tommy's head, I'll clap his ass on sight."

"That's what I am talking about," said Kane, "ya'll know ever since he got down with Rich and them cats from Harlem, he's been trying to take over the block, but it isn't happening.

"This shit is wack yo. Mark and them was straight gangsters. Tommy's crew couldn't have killed them just like that. Maybe one at a time, but not all at once. Yo, on the real, you know what I think right? It was a mob hit," said Jahiem shaking his head in agreement with his own theory.

"Man! Shut the fuck up," said Shamel, and everybody started laughing. So far Ty could tell that none of his friends knew what had really happened. Everybody knew that Tommy and El had been beefing over the block for the past couple of months, so automatically all fingers pointed at Tommy, since Mark and them was part of El's crew, Tommy already had a reputation for being off the hook and he had everything under his belt from shooting people for not buying coke from him, to beating up police. So something like this could be right up his alley.

"Ya'll gonna be here for a minute?" Ty asked fanning smoke from his face. He had only been in the building for a few minutes and the smoke was killing him. He was ready to bounce.

"Yeah probably" said Kane.

"I'm going to the block. I'll be right back."

Ty was on a mission. He had to find out the story behind his friends murders. How could this have happened? This was their block. They ran the drugs in this area for as far back as he could remember. Everybody knew what the team was about, so what's gonna happen now? Will Tommy take over? How is he still walking around if he is the prime suspect? Damn! Where the fuck is the rest of the team? Worm and Chris are the main gunners for El beside Mark. I know they'll handle this shit. How can I get my hands on a gat? All of these thoughts were running through Ty's mind as he walked to the block. He couldn't stop thinking about how they all got caught slipping. Did they have their burners on them when they got shot? If they did, what happen?

The murders of Terrell, Mark and Bobby affected the entire SoundView projects. Nothing would ever be the same. 1988 was the last year of sponsored hustling. There were no more restrictions on who could sell drugs and who couldn't. The rules of the game had changed, not only in Sound View projects but also all over New York. The days of having to be "Okayed" to hustle was gone and the days of the inexperience freelance hustler had begun... The streets would never be the same and neither would its participants.

Kane and Shamel

Ty sat at his mother's kitchen table and started counting the money he just collected from off the block. Once he was sure his count was correct, he began to bottle up the two ounces of coke he had just picked up from his new connect on consignment.

Over the past few months he had built his clientele up real nice. He now had direct access to a stable source of cocaine who had good coke and would match what ever he brought. Things were looking well for Ty. He had branched off from the rest of the hustlers on the block and he hooked up with a crack head that rented him her apartment to use as a crack spot for forty dollars a day. Ty didn't mind giving her the money because he knew that he would make it right back. All the heads that copped from the hustlers on the block came up to Barbara's house to get high anyway. So Ty figured as long as he was there with his product, they wouldn't have to go back out once they came in until they needed more money.

By him having some of the best crack out there and a stable location, his product was moving like water. He sold about 500 nickel bottles a day, and he didn't have to chase or out hustle anybody to do it. All he had to do was sit in Barbara's house until his packs were gone. Things picked up fast, and since he needed some help, he put both of his friends Lite and Man down with him. This way one of them could always be around.

Everything was falling into place for him. Money was coming in daily and that kept him in new gear everyday. As far as he knew he was doing it how it was supposed to be done. He was 16 years old and for his age he was living, but he still wondered how long it would take for him to really blow up. He wanted to shine like all the Boss Players he heard stories about and seen when he went down to Harlem. For years he heard tales of the young street players and he wanted to be apart of that history. He would sit around and daydream about how things would be once he was full blown. He knew that his time was coming, and when it did, he would make sure that he was remembered as one of the best to ever do it. And if things kept going at this pace, it wouldn't be too much longer before he would be floating up 8th Ave in his Benz with access to the world. But until then, he had to keep working.

After placing the bottles into a paper bag and stashing them back in his room, Ty picked up the phone and dialed a number.

"Hello, may I speak to Danny?"

"Who's this Ty?" Danny asked sounding half sleep.

"Yeah, Yo! I'll be ready at nine so come see me."

"Is it the same thing?" asked Danny.

"Yeah," Ty replied.

"I got you kid," Said Danny.

They hung up the phone and Ty called Kane "What's up nigga!" Ty said when he heard Kane answer the phone.

"What's up," Kane replied. "Are you still going?"

"That's why I'm calling you, be ready in ten minutes, you know if we don't get down there early, we'll be standing out side the park."

"I'm ready now, Yo! What's up with Shamel? Is he trooping with us or what?" asked Kane.

"No, he said he was gonna chill with Christine, We'll hook up with him when we come back."

"So let's bounce."

19

"I'm calling an O.J. right now. Meet me in front of the building," said Ty ending the conversation and hanging up the phone.

Ten minutes later Ty and Kane were in a Lincoln Town car headed to 155th and 8th avenue. The Entertainment Classic Basketball Tournament had just begun in Harlem and that was the place to be in the summer on the weekdays in New York. Everybody who was somebody would come through showing off their jewelry and cars. Beamer's and Benz's would be in all flavors, doubled parked everywhere. That made all the gold digging chicks and wonna be gold digging chick's come out in packs. Everybody was trying to be seen but only the elite would be recognized.

"Yo, what's up with you and Sha fucking with Maxine and Christine every night asked Kane with a smirk on his face, breaking the silence in the car. "I hope ya'll niggas ain't falling in love on me or nothing like that."

"Naw nigga not me," Ty said smiling but really wondering if that was true.

Him and Sha had been dealing with the two sisters for about three months now and for the past month they had been going to the girl's house every night. Between trying to build his spot up and messing with Maxine, his free time was becoming very limited. If he wasn't trying to make some money. Max wanted him with her and as of late he had been feeling the same way. She always made him feel wanted and by doing that his feelings had grown for her a lot since they met. But no way in the world would he admit that to Kane or anybody else, at least not right now.

"I don't know," said Kane shaking his head. "Ya'll two niggas have been sneaking off every night fucking with them chicks, you haven't even been fucking with Tanisha since you got with Maxine and she was your heart."

"How you know that?" Ty asked as if Kane didn't know what he was talking about.

"I know because she came on the block yesterday and she told me that she hasn't spoken to you in a week and she hasn't seen you in two weeks, what's up with that?" Kane asked like he had made his point.

"Man, on the real, I'm not feeling Tanisha no more. She isn't on my level. And the only reason why you haven't seen me fucking around with my other slides is because I've been trying to get this paper," said Ty grabbing the print of the knot of money in his front pants pocket.

"Yeah! You can save that shit for somebody who doesn't know your ass. I know you nigga. You just hooked on some older pussy and now you're open." Said Kane, "Plus you haven't been getting no money chillin up in Maxine's house, unless she's paying your little ass to fuck her, or her moms, or somebody else in that house is an undercover crack head," said Kane. Then he busted out laughing. Ty knew he was right and he started laughing with his best friend.

They got out the car on 155th street in front of the Blimpies across the street from the park. The crowd was already forming and it was still an hour before game time. While Ty was checking out a couple of girls walking by in their mean colored spandex and matching 54-11 Reeboks. Kane went into the store to get him a forty once of old English. Ty couldn't stand alcohol, but Kane lived for his beer. When kane came out the store, they walked across that street into the park.

In the next twenty minutes the park was packed, you had chrome rims shining and music blasting out of every car and jeep that drove by. Boss players from every borough in New York rolled into the park, some of them with bags full of money so they could place bets on the games. Girls were posted up around the park in packs trying to score. Some of the females names in the park rang more bells on the streets than some balers, simply because of their past or present relationships. The females in that circle weren't dealing with just anybody, so if you got in and held up with one of them, that could be a big plus for an up and coming player. Especially players who wanted fame behind their name like Kane and Ty.

It was said that a player would know what level of the game he was on by the caliber of women that was checking for him to be honest; there was no better place in New York than Harlem to find out exactly where you stood.

Walking through the crowd, Ty saw Kim and her girlfriend Tawana from out of Throgs Neck projects. Kane had been chasing after Kim all last summer but for some reason they never hooked up. He was crazy about the girl, and Ty saw this as the perfect opportunity to get Kane back for putting him on the spot about Maxine.

"Yo! Kane, check out your girl Kim," Ty said nodding his head in her direction.

Kane's eyes lit up at the sound of Kim's name. "You know I got to go check my wife out," he said smiling walking to her.

Mister I don't love them hoes he would hear about this the whole ride home, Ty thought to himself and smiled.

So they made their way through the crowd towards Kim and Tawana. Kane had spotted Jamal from hunts point entering the park. Jamal was a shit talker. Kane had a few words with him and his peoples a couple months back at Stevenson High School, but the police rolled before anything could really jump off. This was the first time that he had seen Jamal since their last encounter and Kane wasn't about to let him slide.

"Ty! Isn't that that bitch ass nigga Jamal over there?" Kane asked already knowing the answer. Not waiting for a response to his question. Kane walked over to Jamal and punched him in his face. Jamal hit the floor and never recovered. Kane and Ty stomped and punched him into unconsciousness. Kim and Tawana ran over and pulled them off him and walked them off into the park.

"Kane, what's wrong with you? You stay in some shit," Kim said, staring at him shaking her head. She liked Kane, but the way he was always in beef with somebody was the main reason she always procrastinated when it came to them getting together. It seemed like every time she came out side, she heard about Kane and his boys doing something to somebody, and she feared that all of that would catch up to him. She had already went through losing someone that she loved to the streets when her boyfriend was killed two years ago and she never wanted to experience that pain again.

"Boo, don't sweat that, he ain't nobody," Kane said, now smiling again as if nothing had happened. "What's up with you baby girl?"

"I think ya'll should leave. That kid might come back and try to do something stupid," Kim said with concern and experience in her voice.

"Fuck that nigga, he isn't about nothing. Let's go watch the game," Kane said dismissing Kim's suggestion and they walked to the court.

The game was full of excitement. Marcy's All-Stars were playing and they had some new young kid running the point guard position that the announcer duke named the Future. The boy had game. He ran circles around who ever tried to guard him and performed tricks with the ball while doing it. The crowd loved him.

The fourth quarter had just begun when Ty noticed the crowd spreading out by the entrance of the park. Jamal had came back with about twenty of his boys. They were deep and Tyvon automatically began to wonder how the hell they would get out of this one. Kim was right, they should have left. Now what he thought would make them look soft in front of the girls was making a lot of sense.

Jamal and his crew were now splitting up into groups and they were searching the crowd Ty looked over to Kane who looked like he was having the most important conversation of his life and decided that this was time to wake him up out of his trance.

"Kane, Jamal just came back in the park with his peoples," Ty said hoping that Kane would have a better answer to this problem than he did.

"Fuck them niggas! They frontin, they ain't gonna do shit," said Kane and he continued talking to Kim.

"Yo! Kane, them niggas might be strapped," Ty said hoping that mentioning a gun might make Kane think abut the consequence of trying to impress the girls.

"Kane, ya'll should leave," said Kim. "Watch this, come on Ty let's go see what's up!"

He said with a dead serious look on his face.

"Fuck it," Ty said shrugging his shoulders like he didn't care what they did. He was hoping that Kane's act of defiance was really an illusion that would lead to their getaway and not one of his "I don't give a fuck about nothing" plans.

Just as they were about to walk over to Jamal and his crew, somebody had tapped Ty on his shoulder. When he turned around he saw one of the Jamaican guys that sold weed from around his block.

"What's up Face?" Ty asked, wondering what the fuck Face had tapped him for since they had never spoken to each other before.

"Don't worry bout nothing, I'm here," Face said in a deep west Indian accent while lifting up his shirt flashing the handle of the revolver tucked in the waist band of his pants. Ty shook his head in agreement and then he told Kane about what Face had just showed him.

"Man fuck that, if he's gonna look out for us tell him to pass off" said Kane, Ty went and did just that. Face tried to hold out at first but Ty wouldn't let up. He could sense that Face was getting nervous from the amount of pressure that he was applying, but he couldn't figure out why. After a few more seconds, Face finally folded and gave Ty the gun.

"I'll give it right back" Ty said, walking back over to Kane to let him know that they were straight.

"Give me the burner," said Kane.

"Nope, I got this."

"So let's go handle our business," said Kane walking towards Jamal.

By this time all of Jamal's boys had regrouped and were standing at the entrance of the park. They hadn't seen Tyvon or Kane when they walked through the park so they must have thought that they had left. As soon as Ty got with in 15 feet of Jamal, he stepped in front of Kane, "What's up nigga? Is there a problem?" he yelled out.

Jamal looked up, and him and his crew started to rush towards Ty and Kane. Ty immediately pulled out the gun, pointed it at Jamal and pulled the trigger, "Click! Click!" What the fuck, Ty said to himself looking at the gun.

Everybody started running out the park at the sight of Ty pulling out his gun, but the gun didn't go off when he squeezed the trigger. Some of Jamal's boys noticed what had happened and started running back towards Kane and Tyvon.

Kane grabbed Ty's arm and they ran out of the park across the street into the Polo grounds housing projects. Luckily they were able to make it into a building without Jamal or any of his boys seeing them. Once they were in the buildings they ran up nine flights of stairs before stopping. Both Kane and Tyvon were trying to figure out what had happened.

"Yo! What the fucks wrong with this shit," Ty asked, trying to catch his breath before popping the chamber open on the 357 revolver. "Man, this shit is empty" Ty realized that he should have checked to see if the gun was loaded when Face passed it to him.

"That fucking Jamaican bastard tried to get us killed," said Kane. "Wait till we get back on the block, I'm gonna bust his shit."

"Word up, we definitely gonna see that nigga," said Ty, thinking about who he could get some bullets from to see if his new gat worked. Face had tried to play him by giving him an empty gun, so there was no chance of him getting it back. Especially if it worked.

"Let's get up outta here, we have to call Sha so he'll know what's going on. I don't want him to get caught slipping if Jamal and them try to roll," Kane said walking down the steps.

They were walking up Eighth Avenue trying to catch a cab, when they spotted Fat Danny pulling up to a red light in his new black on black 740 BMW. Ty stepped into the street to flag him down.

Ty knew that seeing Danny at this moment was a blessing. He could take care of all his business in one shot. Within an hour, not only would he have 125 grams of pure fish-scale, but he would also have some bullets for his gun.

Back on the block, Shamel waited impatiently in front of Kane's building for him to arrive. "Where the fuck are these niggas at?" He just had another fight with Slim and he was ready to take things to the next level.

Him and Slim had been going at it off and on for the past few months. Shamel didn't like any of the guys that Slim hung out with, and for that season alone he didn't like Slim. Shamel didn't want Slim to come on the block for no reason what so ever and since Slims girl and children lived in Kane's building that was a problem. Every time they saw each other they would fight. Only a month earlier, Ty had to break up a scuffle between the two, and usually something like that was unheard of but since Slim was cool with him and Kane they didn't jump in. Kane had even tried to dead the beef but Shamel wasn't trying to hear it. And since Sha was his man more than Slim, Kane began to take sides.

Shamel had been waiting in front of the building for about an hour, when he saw Fat Danny's Beamer pulling up.

"Where the fuck ya'll niggas been?" Shamel asked showing signs of anger when they got out the car.

"Yo! We just set it off at the Rucker on that nigga Jamal from Hunts Point. I told you, you should have come with us," Kane said like Shamel had missed out on the best thing in the world.

"Word! I'm feeling that. But yo, I just got it on with Slim again and its about time I put some heat in his ass, because he must think it's something sweet about me," Sha said, but not mentioning that he had started the fight with Slim for the hundredth time.

"What ever you want to do. You know how I get down. We can light his ass up tonight," Kane said with a glitter in his eyes, thinking about the gun Ty had on his waist and the box of bullets that Fat Danny had just given him.

"Now that's what I'm talking about," said Shamel smiling, showing his gold teeth. They all walked in the building and went to Kane's house. On the way up stairs, Ty showed Shamel the gun that he had got from Face. Then he told him everything that had happened from them stomping out Jamal, to Kane acting like Mr. Lover man with Kim. After swapping war stories they went to the roof to test the gun.

"Go head nigga, it's yours right? So shoot the motherfucker," said Shamel.

"Don't rush me, I'm gonna do it," said Ty, pointing the gun up in the air and pulling the trigger, Boom! Boom! Boom! The roar of the 357 magnum awoke the night.

"Damn! Don't shoot off all the fucking bullets," Kane said holding his hands over his ears, looking at Ty.

"I had to make sure it worked."

Come on lets go to my crib so I can get my burner. I want to smoke that nigga Slim tonight," said Shamel.

Kane knew that Shamel was serious about what he said and even thought he was gonna go with him, he didn't want Ty to have no parts in it. Tyvon was the baby of the bunch and Kane knew he would be down for what ever, but he also knew that if they killed Slim tonight, and Ty was there, there wouldn't be no turning back. He would have to finish the game and Kane didn't want to put Ty in that position. Ty was like a little brother and despite all of the things that they did together; he still felt the need to look out for him when he could. Kane planned on getting the gun from Ty and him and Shamel could handle this together. Alone.

The Block is Hot

Walking through the door with two shopping bags full of clothes, Tyvon hurried into his room to escape the interrogation process that he was sure would accure if his mother saw him coming in the house with more new clothes that she didn't give him money to buy. For the past few weeks he had been going shopping everyday and even though he was stashing most of his new gear at Kane's house, his moms was still becoming suspicious. She had already threaten to kick him out of the house if she found out that he was selling drugs and since he wasn't ready to move out just yet, he was trying to be extra careful.

All he wanted to do was take a quick shower and get dressed without hearing his mothers mouth. He was going to the Jam in the Big Park tonight and he was pressed for time. Kane, Shamel and a few others would meet him down stairs in a half hour. Lite was finishing up the rest of the bundles that they had in the spot and he would catch up with them in the park when he was done. The weather was nice and Tyvon knew that everybody was coming out tonight. After taking his shower and getting dressed, Tyvon reached under his pillow, grabbed his gun and headed for the door.

It was ten o'clock and the park was jumping. Cars were double and triple parked on the streets and more were pulling up. Most of the guys in the park were from the area but the girls came from all over. Big Paul and his crew had dropped in for a few minutes and had already talked some girls into leaving with them. Fresh had just pulled up in his new white on white drop top Beamer followed by some of his boys from Castle Hill Projects and they were chilling in front of the park talking to Bridget and her crew from Lafayette. El and Stan were in the back of the park smoking a blunt. As Ty walked passed them, he couldn't help but to think about how strong El was before his crew was murdered. It had been a year since their deaths and so much had changed. Big Paul controlled the majority of the narcotic distribution in Soundview now and that meant El was no longer in power and it showed. Tyvon snapped out of his trance when Lite walked up.

"What' up nigga," Lite said, greeting Tyvon with a five and a hug.

"Aint shit, how we looking?" ask Ty.

"I finished everything about a hour ago, but I went home to get dress," said Lite pulling out a knot of money, passing it to Ty.

"They saying our shit's the bomb."

"I'm gonna open up early tomorrow," said Ty, thinking about all the money that they were missing.

"When ever you come out, come get me," Lite said, before diverting his attention to a girl walking by. Lite gently grabbed her hand. "Damn! You look good," he said making her blush.

"Do your thing," said Ty, watching Lite get ready to put his game down. "I'm bouncing over here with Kane and them."

Tyvon walked through the crowd trying to spot where Kane and the rest of the crew had went. When he finally caught up to them, Man and AB were just walking up.

"What up!" said Ty.

"It's on out here tonight," replied AB, looking at a crew of females dancing in front of them.

"Damn! Girl, I wanna see if you can move like that with something up in you." Shamel shouted at the girls who were getting their party on to the sounds of Rob Boss and Easy Rock.

"Where the fuck are these bitches from?" asked Kane, already trying to pick out which one he was going to try and hook up with. For about three records straight the girls held the full attention of the crowd. When they finally settled down, Shamel and Kane had pushed up on two of them and were able to exchanged numbers.

Everybody was socializing and having a good time. Tyvon was standing by the DJ table flirting with a girl that he just met when Lite walked over and whispered in his ear.

"Maxine is here looking for you. She asked me to find you for her."

Ty quickly exchanged numbers with the girl he was talking to and when he walked away, he gave the phone number to Lite to hold for him while he went to talk to Maxine.

"What's up? Mister busy body?" Maxine asked smiling, reaching out to give Ty a hug and kiss as he approached.

"You didn't tell me you were coming out here tonight."

"I wasn't, but I came to get my man, "said Maxine trying her best to persuade Ty into leaving with her. "You ready?"

Tyvon had planned on hanging out with his boys tonight but for some reason he couldn't work himself up to tell her that. He wanted to leave with her but if he did, what would he tell his crew. Fuck it! I'll just tell them I'm bouncing with Max. Who cares what they'll think? Or better yet, I'll just tell them that I scooped me a new shorty and I'm sliding off. Yeah! That'll work, he thought to himself.

"Boo! I'll be right back, let me go tell Kane and them that I'm leaving."

As he was walking back over towards his crew, he spotted Slim and a few of his boys standing with El and Stan near the entrance of the park. Ty knew that Shamel hadn't seen Slim since their last fight a couple of weeks ago, but during that time frame, Shamel and Kane had shot two of Slim boys and that spelled trouble.

"Damn!" Ty said to himself thinking about Maxine and hoping that he could get back over to tell her to leave before anything set off. As soon as he got to Kane and Shamel, he told them that Slim was there.

"You strapped right?" Kane asked Ty.

"Of course," Ty replied flashing the handle of his snub nose 357 that he concealed under his shirt.

Ty knew that he was the only one out of the crew who was packing so leaving with Maxine was now definitely out of the picture. He was cool with Slim and would try to stop any problems from occurring, but if Slim or any of his people tried to move on Shamel or Kane he would hold it down for the crew and wouldn't think twice about pulling the trigger.

"Lets get out of here so I can get my burner," said Shamel.

Kane made sure that everybody that came with them was there, and then they all walked towards the exit. To Tyvon's surprise, Slim and all of the guys that were with him were gone. They had moved from where they were standing and he couldn't spot them anywhere in the crowd. Maybe they bounced. Ty thought as he made his way to Maxine, still scanning the crowd.

"Yo boo, something's about to jump off and I want you to go home."

"So if something is about to happen out here, why don't you leave with me," Maxine asked, trying to figure out why he would want to be somewhere in danger instead of being somewhere safe with her.

"I can't, but I promise we'll hangout all day tomorrow, alright?' Before Maxine could speak, Tyvon cut her off. "I'll call you when I get in the house," said Ty walking away giving her no time to respond or debate.

Just as he walked over to Kane, Maxine screamed "Tyvon!" She was the first to see the three guys in the dark colored hood sweaters pulling out their guns aiming and firing in the direction where Ty and his friends were standing. Pop! Pop! Pop! Pop! Pop! The sound of automatic gunfire sent the crowd scrambling, Ty wasn't able to see who was shooting at them but he was able to locate each shooter from the flash coming out of the muzzles of their guns. Ty fired off rapid shots in their direction. Boom! Boom! Boom! Boom! Everybody was running out of the park and the sound of gunfire now took the place of music. Ty took off running with the crowd and after several seconds the gunfire finally stopped. He could see Kane and the rest of his crew ahead of him and from the looks of things everybody was still together and nobody was hit. After running another half block. Ty caught up to them and they all stopped running.

"Yeah! My nigga, that's the way we do things," Shamel said excitedly hugging Ty.

"Did anybody get hit?" asked Kane.

"I don't know," Ty replied. "I couldn't see who was shooting at us, so I just kept firing in the direction where I saw the sparks from their guns. I saved two bullets in case they tried to chase up."

"You did everything you was suppose to do, now lets get the fuck outta here before we get locked up. We'll get up tomorrow," said Kane and they all split up and went home.

It was eleven o'clock in the morning and Ty was up with hopes of getting rid of the rest of his work before six so he could chill with Max tonight like he promised. Him and Maxine talked on the phone for about two hours last night planning their day and he knew that if anything derailed their plans he wouldn't hear the end of it.

Sitting at the edge of his bed, he reached over and grabbed his beeper off of his desk and checked his calls. He had three new pages. Two from Tanisha, each with a different number, and one from Fat Danny who had called an hour before her. I'll call Tanisha back later, he thought as he picked up the phone and dialed Danny's number.

"Hello! May I speak to Danny?"

"Yeah, what's up kid? What are you doing?"

"I was about to go to the block, why? What's up?"

"Come down stairs in ten minutes, I want you to take a ride with me."

Forty-five minutes later Ty was in Fat Danny's Beamer and they were riding around in Harlem.

"What have you been up to?" Danny asked Ty while he switched the Brucie B tape that was playing for the new one he just bought.

"I've been chilling, why? What's up? Ty asked trying to figure out where this line of questioning was leading.

"There's a lot of shit floating around about you and your little crew and I want you to know that the shit I'm hearing aint about nothing," said Danny. "Your mans are starting a whole bunch of shit trying to get a name when they should be trying to lay low and make some paper. And to be honest with you, they're only two seconds away from catching a bad decision.

"It isn't' even like that," replied Tyvon defensively," Shit be jumping off and when it does, we handle it, And so for as us getting chips, I'm still doing my thing so that aint a problem," said Ty, like if he was making a million dollars a day and Danny wasn't the one supplying him with the drugs he was selling.

"Listen here man; you haven't begun to touch any real paper yet," said Danny now turning down the music in the car. "Yeah! I'll give it to you, you're trying to get some shorts and you're doing a lot better than most kids but if you keep getting into bull shit beefs because of your boys, you'll be dead before you get to reach you full potential. Don't get me wrong, I'm not saying that your team is soft because that's far from true. But your peoples have definitely been stepping out of their league lately. Yeah, I heard about Kane swinging on chicks from the boulevard but you see what happen right? Kane's girl got shot in the process. And don't think that nobody knows that him and Shamel were the ones that killed that dude at the Whitestone.

What type of shit was that? I heard they shot the guy because Shamel wanted his girl. Shit like that is wack. Ty, I'm not telling you not to get down with your boys when ever there's a problem, but I am telling you if it doesn't make dollars, it don't make sense. Stay out of this bullshit and focus on getting your money right.

They drove around and talked for two more hours, then Danny dropped Ty off on the block. Everything Danny had said made sense, especially the money part, but Ty knew that the bond between him Kane and Shamel was more than a friendship, they were brothers and people failed to understand that. All three of them respected and treasured true friendship, but it was their respect for loyalty that kept them close. They all stood up for each other no matter what the cause. If one had a problem, then they all had a problem, and everybody knew that. So basically it really didn't matter if Ty was directly involved with a beef or not, in everyone else's eyes he would be in it, so he had to be ready for what ever came his way. Damn, only if they would chill out for a minute and focus on getting some paper with me. We could be able to lock shit down. Ty thought to himself, knowing that the odds against that happening anytime soon was one in a million. He had tried to make some money with Kane in the past and things didn't work out.

He had given Kane a few packs to flip, so he could get on his feet, and everything was looking good in the beginning. Within two days Kane had doubled his money, but instead of him going to re up again, he went shopping and spent all of his money on clothes. Then he had the nerve to get mad at Ty because he wouldn't lend him some more money to get back on. They didn't speak to each other for a week behind that.

And for Shamel, his excuse was that he was out on bail and didn't want to catch another case. Ty couldn't understand that one because it seemed like every other day. Shamel was shooting at somebody, and it don't take a genus to know that that wasn't the best way to stay out of jail. Ty had come to the conclusion a long time ago that the both of them were just lazy. They would rather take it then make it. But Ty knew once he started to blow up they would wake up and get with the program. Everybody loves a winner, Ty thought smiling as he knocked on Lites door.

"Where the fuck have you been?" Lite asked, letting Ty into the apartment.

"I went down town with Fat Danny," Ty said, handing Lite a paper bag with five hundred vials of crack in it.

"Yo! There was crazy loot out here this morning, everybody was looking for us," said Lite, looking in the bag. "We could have finished at least half of this shit already, if not all of it."

"Damn! I knew it was gonna be like that. I tried to get out here early, but Danny came and got me," Ty said, knowing that once a hustler had missed that fiend money it was gone. You couldn't make it up, All you could do was wait and be prepared for the next rush that was sure to come.

"A yo! I'm gonna get outta here about six o'clock. I have to take care of a few things and I'm gonna need you to help me collect some shorts," Ty said, keeping in mind his date with Maxine.

"Come on man! That ain't nothing, Just tell me who and how much."

"Good looking out."

Their date was beautiful. Maxine had planned everything perfectly. She was tired of them being cooped up in the house every night with Shamel and her sister, so she made sure that tonight was different. Christine had given her the run down on a few places they might want to go but she already had everything mapped out. Maxine had been on her share of dates as well. So she basically knew where and how she wanted the evening to go down. The night went perfect. They went to the movies, then they picked up some seafood from City Island, and after they ate, they ended the evening at the Capri Hotel. Ty loved it. Besides him dipping into his re-up money to keep the O. J on hold the whole night, so he could impress Maxine, he had no regrets.

Back in the projects, the money was flowing. Big Paul's yellow top crew was taking in most of the cash as usual. His team didn't maintain their status because they had the best product on the block, or because they forced other hustlers out of business, but because they were consistent with providing what they had.

On the other side of the projects, Lite had sold all of the packs he had, plus he had already collected the money that Tyvon had asked him to. As far as he was concerned, business was done, so he went and hooked up with the rest of the crew in the pizza shop. When Lite entered the pizza shop, A.B and Lil Tray were both concentrating on beating each other in a game of Street Fighter.

"What's good?" asked Lite.

"What's up?" A.B replied, rapidly pushing buttons not bothering to turn around to see who he was speaking to.

The game was over in another two moves and Lil Tray was jumping up and down in excitement over his victory.

"Yeah! Nigga, I told you, you couldn't fuck with me," yelled Tray.

"Why don't you sit your little cheating ass down," A.B. said half jokingly, turning to greet Lite.

"Don't get mad because I busted your ass three games in a row," said Tray laughing.

"I thought you were supposed to be at camp?" Lite asked, remembering the academic trip that Tray was accepted to go on with the rest of his schools top students.

"We just came back today. I didn't even go home yet," Tray replied, pointing down, showing Lite his bags that were on the side of the video machine.

"You need to take your little fat ass home," A.B. said, then he purposely changed the subject. "Anyway! I know you heard about what Man and them did to that kid that Diane was fucking with right?"

"Nah! What happen?" asked Lite

"They stamped his ass out and took his car."

"Word," Lite said excitedly," where they at?"

"They went to the back of the projects," said A.B

"I'm going back there, I wanna push that whip," said Lite, rushing out of the pizza shop. "Hold up!" shouted Tray, picking up his bags running behind Lite.

They caught up to Man and the rest of the crew with in minutes, everybody was in the parking lot smoking weed, watching Man and Tone search the Volvo that they just jacked.

"What' up nigga," Lite said, walking up on Man who was sitting in the drivers seat. "You know I got to push this joint," said Lite, admiring the new Volvo like it was his dream car.

"Do your thing, but don't get knocked trying to O.D." Man said getting out of the car handing Lite the keys, "you know how you are." Everybody laughed.

"Go head with that bull shit, I got this," said Lite getting into the car, he leaned the seat back, turned up the music and was about to pull off when a car entered the parking lot with its high beams on. Because of the bright lights, he couldn't see what kind of car was approaching so he jumped back out the car and walked away just in case it was the police. Suddenly the car slowed to a stop and a guy wearing black army fatigues stepped out firing , BLAP, BLAP, BLAP, BLAP, BLAP, BLAP, BLAP, Everybody took off running splitting up as they ran into the projects. A.B followed Lite into his building. Just as they found refuge in the building, they heard some one yelling "Nooo!", then a string of automatic gun fire, BLAP, BLAP, BLAP, BLAP, BLAP, BLAP, BLAP. The silence after the last burst of shots left an echo in the ears and hearts of Lite and A.B.

"Lite get the burner," said A.B, out of breath fondling for his asthma pump.

"I think somebody got hit."

Lite all of a sudden had a feeling of frustration rush through his body because he didn't have access to a gun of his own. Ty would usually leave the heat with him when ever he was hustling, but since he went out, he took it with him. "Ty got it" said Lite flatly.

"Damn!" said A.B. trying to figure out a quick solution to even out their problem.

"Yo! You really think somebody got hit?" asked Lite.

"I hope not, but we better go find out."

"Come on."

As they walked out of the building they could see a crowd gathering up in the parking lot. Some people were crying, while others looked on in silence. A. B. and Lite began to run towards the crowd to see what had happened and when they got there, they were in just as much shock as everyone else. Man was sitting on the floor drenched in blood crying, holding Lil Tray's bullet riddled body, Tray was dead, He never made it home from his trip or out of the parking lot before the streets claimed him.

"He didn't have a chance," said Man looking up at Lite, Blood from Tray's body soaked his clothes as it drained into the street. "He ran behind me but he couldn't keep up."

The police arrived and several minuets later the ambulance came. The paramedics didn't attempt to work on Tray, he was hit at least seven times in the chest and back area, and twice in the head. They pronounced him dead on the scene. The police took Man in for questioning and they closed off the area. Detectives and uniform police were all over and it wasn't long before they were harassing who ever walked by. The block was hot.

"Yo, come with me to my crib. I have to call Ty so he wont come over here and get caught up in this bullshit."

By the time Tyvon got his wake up call in the morning, his pager was on over flow and most of the calls were from Lite. Something had happened. He could feel it. He immediately picked up the phone and dialed Lite's number.

"What happen?" Ty asked, hearing Lite's voice on the other line.

Lil Tray got killed last night."

"Get the fuck outter here!" said Ty, in disbelief, picturing Lil Tray running around the projects playing box ball. Tray was only thirteen years old, and wasn't into any street activity. What could have happened? Ty asked himself.

"What happen? "Ty asked before catching himself and remembering Fat Danny's number one rule. Don't ever talk street over the phone. "As a matter of fact don't answer that, I'll meet you on the block in a few minutes," he said then hung up the phone.

"Boo! What happened?" asked Maxine sensing that something was wrong.

"Lil Tray got killed last night," Ty replied still in shock sitting on the bed staring at a blank T.V. screen.

"Shamel's little brother?'

"Yeah."

"For real, what happen?"

"I don't know, let's get dressed, we gotta go."

After dropping Maxine off at her house, Tyvon went and hooked up with Lite and A.B. When Lite told him everything that had happened, Ty couldn't believe that. Tray was dead over something so simple. The murder rate around the hood was escalating and it seemed like the ages of the people getting killed was decreasing with each victim. The murder of Lil Tray showed just how much times were changing. Just a year ago, something like this was unheard of in Ty's young world. If some one would have asked him two years ago to describe exactly how he felt when ever someone he knew was murdered, he couldn't begin to answer that question truthfully, because he never experienced such a situation. But if he was asked that same question right now, his answer would flow naturally with out thought. Times had changed, and they changed fast.

Tyvon couldn't help but to reflect back on the deaths of Terrell, Mark and Bobby. He knew if they were still alive, it was a good chance that Tray's death would have been prevented. They didn't allow any bull shit on the block, mainly because they didn't want any of the extra police attention that came with it. Even though they only kept order around the project to maintain an unthreatened illegal flow of cash, order was still being kept. But since their deaths, it was open season. Thinking of this, Tyvon began to lose a lot of respect for most of the older guys who claimed that they were reppin the hood in the absence of Mark and them, because in all reality, all they was doing was living off the strength of the dead. They weren't really trying to step up.

It was weird, because on any given day, you could walk around the block and hear a number of people telling stores about guys who were no longer around, or how things would be if this one, or that one was still alive. But these same people who seemed to thrive off the memories of the past wasn't willing to do what had to be done to keep what they claimed to believe in alive. Ty knew once he got the chance, he would restore everything that was lost in the hood. Everybody who wanted to live, but didn't have the heart to push, could live their dreams through him. The passing of the torch was officially in effect, and at that moment Ty knew what had to be done and who had to do it.

Changing of the Guard

The remaining weeks of summer passed quickly after Lil Trays death, School was already back in session and for the average teenager that meant that the fun and relaxation of the summer was officially over. But for Tyvon, all it meant was that flossing season was open. He only went to school to flirt with the girls and to show off his new gear, then he was gone. School didn't make much sense to him any more. All he saw was people going to school, some graduating, but everybody struggling to live a decent life when it was all over. He knew that he made more money in an hour then the average working person made in a week, and that was one of the main reasons he never worked a legit job, and didn't ever plan on working one. In Tyvon's eyes, if all school did was help a person find a job in the future; it was a waste of his time. He felt as long as he could read, count, and write, fuck school. The only connections he wanted with school or a job, was schooling motherfuckers on how to get some real chips when he owned his own business in a few years. But as for now, he was still trying to come up so his only focus was on mastering the game and surviving while doing it.

One day during the early afternoon, Kane went to Maxine's house looking for Ty. He was on his way to Webster Project to meet Wendy at her crib, and he wasn't about to go over there empty handed. He needed a gat.

Kane rang the doorbell, and to his surprise Maxine's mother answered the door. He knew that Ty was usually at Max's house everyday around this time, but he didn't know if Maxine's mom knew that.

"Hi, Ms. Rivera, is Maxine home?" Kane asked nervously. "Now you know you're not looking for my daughter," said Ms. Rivera, "If you want Tyvon, just ask for him. Don't be scared Poppy, I don't bite," said Ms. Rivera smiling.

"Huh! Um, yeah I'm looking for Tyvon," Kane said forcing a smile on his face.

"Come in poppy, he's in the back room," said Ms. Rivera, before calling out to Ty letting him know that he had company.

Kane entered Maxine's room, and Ty was sitting a the edge of the bed, in nothing but his boxer shorts, and Maxine was laying down in the bed watching T.V. "Damn! Nigga, you got it like that now huh?" Kane asked gesturing to how relaxed Ty was in Maxine's house, even with her moms around.

"You know how I do," Ty replied with a smirk on his face, giving Kane a five.

"Yeah, I see," Kane said looking around the room checking out all of Maxine's clothes, and even noticing some of Ty's things hanging up in her closet. Damn, She got my little man whipped, he thought to himself. I see you got some real in house pussy jumping off around here."

"Are you jealous?" asked Maxine in her most sarcastic voice. She knew that Kane didn't like Ty spending more time with her than he did with him, and now seeing just how much Ty was taking care of her, he was really heated. This nigga needs a girl so he could stay the hell out of mines, Maxine thought to herself.

"Jealous of what?" asked Kane defensively. But before he could go on, Ty interrupted him.

"Take off your jacket and chill for a minute," said Ty, stopping the argument before it started.

"Naw! I gotta bounce, I just came by to pick up one of them burners you just copped," said Kane. "I'm hooking up with that girl Wendy I met at the jam and I wanted to get strapped before I went to her crib."

"That ain't no problem," said Ty reaching under the pillow grabbing the 9 mm Glock that he always left at Max's house. "Take this one," said Ty passing him the gun.

"Good lookin," Kane said looking at the gun and checking the clip.

"Yo, Hold on to that as long as you want," said Ty.

"I know nigga. What's mines is yours and what's yours is mine and can't nobody change that," said Kane giving Maxine a look of disgust. She rolled her eyes back at him.

Kane didn't waste anytime heading for the door after getting the gun from Ty. He had been trying to get in Wendy's drawers ever since that night he saw her and her girlfriends dancing at the Jam in the big park last summer and he wasn't about to waste any more time.

"Oh yeah! Lend me some shorts until later, I'll give it back tonight when I pick my money up from my pops," said Kane, remembering that he was low on cash but at the same time wishing that he would have come up with a new line.

"Man you always say that. I ain't seen your pops give you no money since he came home. I told you what you need to do. Stop bullshitting and get your money right."

Ty said, showing signs of anger. He was tired of Kane's lazy ways. Kane didn't want to get a job, and he didn't want to hustle, but he always wanted something.

"Yeah I know, I'm gonna do something this week, that's my word," said Kane, putting on his best, I learned my lesson face.

"How much you need?" asked Ty, staring at Kane. "I'm fucked up so don't get crazy."

"Naw! It ain't even like that, I just need about fifty."

"Don't ask me for shit until you pay me my money back," said Ty, passing him the fifty dollars out of some bills he had on top of the dresser.

"Stop frontin nigga, you know you love me," said Kane smiling, walking out the door counting the money that Ty had just given him. "And Max, take it easy on my man, He's still trying to come up."

"Fuck you Nigga," Maxine yelled and shut the door.

A half hour later Kane was knocking on Wendy's door. She opened the doors standing with only a towel wrapped around her body. She dropped the towel to the floor and smiled as Kane entered the apartment. He immediately greeted her with a long passionate kiss as she led him into her bedroom. It was on.

In Harlem, on 112 Street between St. Nicholas and 7th avenue, Slim was invited to a meeting held by Ced and his associates. Slim and Ced had been friends for years but this was the first time he was ever asked to attend any type of meeting. Usually they would hang out together in clubs, or go out to eat with some girls, but they never dealt with each other on a business level, and even thought Ced hadn't mentioned what they was meeting for, Slim could tell that during this get together some form of business would be introduced or addressed.

Ced pulled into the block right on time in his brand new red twin turbo 300z. He was becoming one of Harlem's young rising stars in the drug game, and it showed from how the other players in the game treated him, to how the streets whispered his name. The boy was blowin up and blowin up fast.

He pulled up beside Slims double parked Acura integra. "Park right over there," Ced said, pointing to a empty parking space. Then he pulled off.

Ced drove over to 115 street, parked his car and walked back to 112 street where Slim followed him to the building in the middle of the block. When they entered the apartment, Ced was happy to see that all of his crew were there not on time, but before time. He was big on a person's punctuality, and his crew knew that he had made a few examples out of people who over looked his seriousness about being on time, or following rules. Once the word got out on how he handled those situations, he no longer had any more problems. "What's good?" asked Ced as him and Slim walked through the door. "What's up!" Stan said. They were in the living room playing Nintendo on the 60" inch T.V. Everybody greeted each other with the usual hand shake and hug, then Ced motioned for Tone to turn the game off. It was time to take care of business.

"Yo! This is the first time that I invited Slim to sit in with us at a meeting, and ya'll know why he's here but he doesn't, so let me get straight to the point. Slim, I want you to get down with our team. I think if you and Stan work together up in the Bronx, we could make a lot of shit happen. Who ever doesn't work for you, will buy work from you, or they won't work at all. It's as simple as that. We're about to make some major moves, and I want to know if you're with us or not, the decision is yours," said Ced, now staring at Slim waiting for his answer.

Slim had been waiting for this moment for a long time, and he was more than ready to get down with Ced's crew. He knew that even though Ced was young, he was a professional, and that meant as long as you played by the rules of the game, you wouldn't have any problem coming up. The amount of money that Slim would make teaming up with Ced would definitely help him take care of his girl, and their three kids like he always wanted to, so there wasn't anything else to think about. "I'm with it, but there's a little problem we have to take care of first," said Slim.

Back around the way, Shamel and some of the crew was hanging around out side of Stevenson High school.

Shamel had dropped out of school two years ago when he was arrested on an attempted murder charge, but he still popped up from time to time just to show his face. Everybody in the school knew him, and he loved the attention that he got whenever he came around. The girls loved him, and the guys feared him. A lot of people actually thought that the girls feared him too, and that was why they acted like they liked him, but if that was the case, you couldn't tell because they all went out of their way to speak to him. In their eyes, he was a local celebrity, and they treated him like a star.

"Hi Shamel," said a group of girls, smiling and waving at him as they walked by. He acknowledged them with a smirk and the nod of his head, then he continued to scan the crowd.

"I don't know what it is, but the chicks be feeling this nigga," A.B. said admiring the girls as they passed wondering why they hadn't spoken to him. "Sha, you gonna have to put me up on your game, Word up!"

"It ain't no game, bitches just love them a real nigga," Shamel said nonchalantly, staying focused on the crowd of students exciting the school. He had came up there today trying to catch up with a girl that he saw the day before, waiting for the bus when he was in a dollar cab. The girl was looking good, and he made it his business to get up to the school the next day so he could meet her. "Damn! Ya'll niggas made me miss her," he said as he watched the crowd separate into groups heading to the bus stops, while others walked or got into cabs.

"Who you talking about," asked Man, not knowing that they were looking for any one particular.

"My future wife," said Shamel.

"Niggas I hear that shit every week from your ass," said Jahiem.

"Word up!" added A.B.

It didn't seem to bother Shamel how many girls he met in a week. The newest one was always his future wife, until he met someone else that interested him.

"Come on, let's get up outta here, I got to meet Christine at the clinic in a half hours," said Shamel looking at his watch.

"The clinic, what's that about?" asked A.B.

"Chris thinks she's pregnant."

"Word! My boy's gonna be a father, get the fuck outta here," said Jahiem excitedly putting his arm around Shamel's shoulder.

"I don't think I'm ready for any kids right now," said Shamel thinking about the responsibility of raising a child. "Besides, I'm already a father," said Shamel with a devilish grin.

"I didn't know you had any kids," said Man, curiously.

"Don't play yourself, who did you think your father is?" said Sahmel, looking at Man and everybody busted out laughing, "Let's get outta here."

Over the next few weeks things were changing rapidly. Kane had practically moved in with Wendy, and ever since Shamel found out that Christine was pregnant, and that she had no plans of having an abortion, he had decided to calm down a little and make some money with Ty.

Tyvon had been waiting for this move for the longest, and everything was working out better than he could have ever imagined. So Tyvon's surprise.

Shamel wasn't nowhere near as lazy as he thought, and on top of that, he was excellent with managing money. Shamel made sure that he saved a certain amount of money every week, and when Ty noticed how fast Shamel was coming up, he started doing the same.

"Ty, I got 1,500 $ to put in this week when you go re-up," said Shamel, taking a knot of money from out of a sneaker box, and tossing it on his bed. "I would've put in

2,500 $ but I had to give Chris some shorts so she could put a deposit down on our new apartment."

"Don't sweat it, this is good, Shit! If we keep moving like this, we'll be copping half a brick in no time."

Since Shamel got down with him, Ty was coming up faster than ever. Instead of buying the same amount of weight like he had been doing for the past three months, he was now able to double his buy. Shamel hadn't been hustling a full three weeks before he started adding a couple hundred towards their re-up money, and that was big. Danny was still doubling what ever he bought so they had managed to stay way ahead of the game, and it was becoming noticeable.

Just a few days earlier, he was talking to Big Paul, and his right hand man Dre. They both made comments about how his spot was blowin up. Even though they made it sound like a compliment, Ty knew that this was a business, and as soon as anybody viewed him as a threat to their daily income, there would be problems. Tyvon was sure that his team was built for what ever was to come their way, and he was more than ready to prove that whenever the time arrived.

"Let me get up outta here so I can get with Danny before he breaks out," said Ty stuffing the money that Shamel just gave him into his pants pocket and heading for the door.

"Break out?" asked Shamel curiously.

"Yeah, he's bouncing to D.C for a few days, and I wanna make sure that we're straight before he leaves."

"Cool, I'll get up with you when you get back."

"Oh yeah, Kane beeped me earlier talking about going to a party tonight that one of Wendy's girlfriends are having on Story Ave, what's up? Are we in there, or what?" asked Ty.

Fat Danny had been selling kilo's of cocaine in Washington D.C. for the past five years through a girl named Tami, that he had met at the hair show in Atlantic City. Tami was directly connected to Raymond Evens, one of D.C.'s biggest drug dealers and through her associations, she was able to put together some major deals from time to time. So when Tami called Danny saying that she had somebody who wanted to buy 15 New York Knicks tickets, he immediately told her that he had them, and that he would call her back in a few hours when he came into town.

Danny and Tami's relationship went beyond just business, so he knew that he would be staying with her in D.C for a few days like he normally did, and he was sure that Ty was going to need something while he was gone, so he called, and told Ty to meet him at his girls house on 132nd and fifth avenue, with in the next hours, Ty arrived at Keisha's house ten minutes after Danny did.

"What's up kid?" said Danny, as he let Ty into the apartment. Keisha walked out of the kitchen with a box of zip lock bags, and handed them to Danny.

"Hey sweetie! Where have you been stranger?" said Keisha, smiling at Tyvon.

"Just chillin, What's up with you?" Ty asked, trying his hardest not to stare at Keisha's figure filling out the tight guess jeans that she was wearing as he walked around the living room.

"Same shit, just a different day," Keisha replied, in her care free way. "Oh I forgot I'm mad at you."

"Why?" asked Ty.

"Because you asked me to hook you up with Veronica, and since she gave you her number, you haven't called. I'm not feeling that."

"It ain't even like that, I've just been busy," Ty said, knowing that he would love to get with Veronica, but at the same time he knew that if he got with her right now, he would be stepping way out of his league. Veronica was Keisha's younger cousin. She was only three years older than Tyvon, but she had been hanging out with Keisha, and all of her girlfriends for years, and their whole crew had a reputation of only dealing with official baller's, and that intimidated Ty. He knew that he was still dealing with short paper, and he wanted to at least be able to produce the things that Veronica was use to having if they hooked up, and right now, he didn't think that was possible without going broke.

"Tell her that I didn't forget about her, I've just been running around trying to take care of my business. I promise I'll give her a ring in a few days."

"Yeah what ever!" said Keisha, waving her hand at him. "We'll see if you call." She said smiling.

"He'll call when he's ready," Danny said, cutting into their conversation, and motioning to Ty to follow him into the bedroom.

"I'll talk to you later," Keisha said to Ty rolling her eyes, openly showing disgust for Danny's rudeness.

"No doubt," said Ty entering the bedroom.

Danny opened the closet, reached inside a duffel bag, and pulled out a zip lock bag full of crack. "Weigh this, it should be 350 grams," said Danny, tossing the bag to Ty. Ty walked over to the triple beam scale that was on the top of the dresser, and weighed the coke. "It's straight," he said, putting the rocks of crack cocaine back into the zip lock bag.

Danny liked Tyvon a lot, so he didn't mind helping him come up. Ty was doing real good for himself, and there was no doubt in Danny's mind that as long as Ty had somebody to guide him, he would achieve much more then the average hustler twice his age, and Danny planned on being his mentor.

"I'll be in D.C. for a few days, but when I come back I'll have a half a brick for you."

"My money ain't like that yet," said Ty, knowing that he would have to go into his stash to buy 250 grams, for Danny to give him to other 250 on consignment.

"Don't sweat that, I got you kid," said Danny, reassuring Ty that he had nothing to worry about. "Just keep doing what you been doing and you'll be alright."

"Good lookin," Ty said excitedly, knowing that this would lead to his big brake.

They talked for another ten minutes before Ty called a cab, and left. When he arrived at Maxine's house, Shamel was already there. They immediately walked into Maxine's room so they could talk in private.

"What's good?" asked Shamel, closing the door behind him.

"Yo! We're about to make some major moves," said Ty excitedly. Before Shamel could ask him what he was talking about, he continued. "Danny is gonna hit us with a half of key when he comes back from D.C."

"Say word!" said Shamel in disbelief but already calculating numbers in his head.

"Once we start rolling like that, it's on," said Ty, "I'm trying to shit on the world."

"Nigga, you ain't saying nothing, I'm gonna have to change my name to Boss Floss the way I'm gonna shine," said Shamel, and they both started laughing.

They both knew once they got that half a key, it wouldn't take them long to double it into a kilo, and when that happened, they would have enough coke to start spreading out, and that meant more money. As long as they kept Danny's money straight, they would be able to get what ever they could handle.

"What's up with Kane?" asked Ty, taking the bag of coke out of the inside pocket of his North face, and putting it in one of Maxine's shoes boxes under her bed.

"I spoke to him about a half hour ago, He's chillin, we're gonna get up with him at the party."

"Cool, what time we leaving?"

"It's nine now, we could leave in about an hour," Shamel said, looking at this watch.

"Yeah! About ten or ten thirty. That'll give me enough time to break Chris off before we bounce so I won't have to hear her mouth."

Shamel and Tyvon arrived at the party around eleven o'clock. They hooked up with Kane and immediately began to get their party on. The place was packed. They were at least two girls to every guy, and more were showing up by the hour.

"Kane, isn't that Tiffany from behind T.S.S over there talking to them two corn balls?" asked Ty, pointing in her direction.

"Yeah, that's her over there with that fat ass," Kane replied. "I just tried to push up on her before ya'll got here but she was trying to act like she's all that now. A bitch gain a few pounds now she don't know how to act."

"Damn! She blew up over the summer like crazy," said Ty, memorized by how good Tiffany was looking.

"Didn't she give you her digits before?" Sahmel asked, knowing that she had, and wondering why Ty never got with her. The girl was bad.

"Yeah, I had her number but Tanisha found it and ripped it up," said Ty, still staring at Tiffany from across the room.

"What! Man listen, I would've beat Tanisha's little ass if she would've made me miss out on a piece of pussy like that," said Kane. "Now I know why you really stopped fuckin with her. And all this time I thought it was because

Max had you whipped." They all started laughing, and before Tyvon could respond to Kane's comment, Shamel was nudging him.

"Speaking of Tanisha, look who's coming our way," said Shamel, nodding in the direction that she was coming from.

Ty looked up, and Tanisha was walking straight towards them. Damn! She's gonna be sweating me all night, he thought to himself. Ty had been ducking her ever since he started seriously going out with Maxine, and even though Tanisha had heard all the rumors about Ty dating this older Puerto Rican girl, she had never heard directly from him that he was in a new relationship, so she kept on insisting that they try to work out their problems.

"What's up ya'll: Tanisha said cheerfully, waving at Kane and Shamel. They both waved back, then she directed her attention to Ty, "And how are you mister?"

"I'm chillin," said Ty flatly still focusing on Tiffany, paying Tanisha no mind.

"Tyvon, we need to talk," said Tanisha, "I'm not felling your new stink little attitude at all," she said openly displaying her anger towards him for his lack of attention.

"That's not my problem." Ty said coldly. Shamel started laughing and Tanisha both angry and embarrassed, walked away with her head down.

Just as she walked off, Tiffany had finished her conversation with the two guys that she had been talking to, and had began walking towards her girlfriends. Ty didn't miss a beat.

"I'll be right back," he said to Kane and Shamel, making his way across the room. Tiffany had been talking to her girlfriends when Tyvon walked up behind her and whispered in her ear. "Let me find out that you have been hiding from me." When she turned and seen who was talking to her, her face lit up with excitement, and she broke into a big smile.

"What's up boo?" she said giving Tyvon a tight hug. "Long time no see."

"Yeah, too long," said Ty, taking a step back, and openly admiring what he was looking at.

Tiffany pulled Ty into a corner so they could continue their conversation in private, but she couldn't help but to notice the girl standing behind Ty staring at them.

"I think you got some company," Tiffany said, gesturing to the girl staring at them figuring that she was standing there for him because she had never saw her before. When Ty looked to see what she was talking about, he was staring right in Tanisha's face. This bitch is crazy, he thought to himself, grabbing Tiffany's hand and walking towards the door.

"Let's go out here so we can kick it without anybody sweating us."

"Yeah, I think we better because your little girlfriend looks like she's ready to start buggin out."

Tyvon and Tiffany walked out into the staircase and resumed their conversation. They both began telling each other about their summer and what they had planned for the winter. Before either of them realized it, they had been talking for more than an hour. I should run back inside for a minute to let Kane and them know where I'm at, Ty thought to himself, but then decided against it. He was really enjoying Tiffany's company, and he didn't want to spoil the mood. Plus he didn't want to take the chance of her thinking he was going back into the party to try to patch things up between him and Tanisha. Oh! Hell no. They know that I wouldn't leave without telling them. Ty thought, looking at the time on his pager. I'll check up on them in a few.

While Tyvon was trying to get his mack on, Shamel was bringing Kane up to date with all of the business moves that him and Ty were making.

"Its about to happen for us and we want you to be apart of everything that we get into," said Shamel looking Kane in the eyes, making sure that he was getting his point across. "But you can't be half stepping."

Kane was fully aware that making money with friends was totally different from just hanging out. If you let it, money could either make or break a relationship, and he learned that from his and Tyvon's past business experience, and that's why he avoided working with them. But seeing how fast Shamel was coming up, it was hard to turn them down. With thoughts of getting left behind, Kane was suddenly ready to take another chance.

"I'm with whatever ya'll wanna do," he said sternly, not breaking their eye contact. "So let's stop talking about it and let's make it happen."

More than satisfied with Kane's response, Shamel gave him a hug. "Lets go find Ty so we can really kick it."

After briefly searching through the party they realized that Ty wasn't in there. They knew that he wouldn't have left with out saying something to them, so they decided to check down stairs to see if he was out side. While waiting for the elevator, they ran into Man, A.B and Jahiem. They had just arrived.

"What's good fam!" said Jahiem.

"Ain't shit," responded Shamel, grabbing hold of the elevator door so it wouldn't close making everybody on it wait until he finished talking.

"I know ya'll ain't bouncing already?" asked A.B.

"Nah, we looking for Ty, so we was going down stairs to see if he was out there," said Kane. "ya'll didn't see him out side when ya'll came up?" asked Shamel, ignoring the impatient looks on the faces of everybody on the elevator.

"Naw, but he could've been down there," said Jahiem. "A lot of people were hanging in front of the building when we came but 5-0 was harassing motherfuckers so we came in from the back."

"Word up, if ya'll strapped be on point down there because the D's are jumping out on everything moving," said Man.

"It would be just our luck to get off the elevator and walk into a bunch of super cops looking for some rec, "said Shamel handing Jahiem his Glock.

"Word up!" Kane said in agreement passing his nine to Man and getting into the elevator "we'll be right back."

When Kane and Shamel got down stairs it was like they went to another party. People were everywhere. In the lobby, sitting on cars, walking back and forth, just enjoying the atmosphere. Everybody was trying to hook up with somebody before the night was over. Coming out of the building Shamel stopped to talk to a couple girls that were calling him while Kane walked over to one of Tiffany's girlfriends. "Jackie, you haven't seen Ty anywhere out here have you?" asked Kane.

"Not out here," she responded. "I seen him earlier, he was talking to Tiffany in the party. That was about an hour ago. You want me to tell him something if I see him?"

"Yeah, tell him that we're upstairs waiting for him," Kane said turning to watch the sky blue M.P.V with the dark tinted windows that was slowly pulling up the ramp. The van was familiar, Damn! I know I seen that ride some where before, Kane said to himself, so he made his way over to Shamel.

"Oh shit! Kane said, instinctively reaching for his gun that he didn't have with one hand and pushing Shamel with the other. Sha! He yelled, seeing Slim jump out of the van with a Mac-10 aimed right at them.

The girls that Shamel had been talking to screamed before the shots went off. Blap! Blap! Blap! Blap! Everybody that was hanging out in front of the building was now scrambling for their lives. The gunshots out weighted the screaming that could be heard blocks away. People pushed and shoved their way back into the building. While others jumped into cars trying to find safety. After another burst of automatic gun fire that seemed to last forever, Slim jumped back in to the van and they sped away.

Seconds after the shooting stopped, Jackie peeped up from behind the parked car that she had found refuge and saw Kane lying on the curb holding his stomach squirming in pain.

He had been shot.

"Kane!" she screamed running over to him. "Hold on boo, you'll be alright," she said holding his hand. "Somebody call an ambulance!"

Kane was in pain from the slugs he took in the stomach, but he was fully conscious.

"Where's Sha? He rasped looking around at the crowd of people staring at him. He didn't recognize any one accept Jackie. "Jackie, go get Jahiem and Man. They're upstairs in the party."

Jackie didn't want to leave Kane by himself in the condition he was in, but she did exactly what he asked her to.

Tyvon didn't hear any of the shots, but his conversation was interrupted by the groups of people that were running up the stairs screaming. "They shooting! They shooting!" Once he made out exactly what was being said, he immediately thought about his boys and jumped up.

"Tiff, stay right here. I'll be back," he said rushing back to the party. Just as Ty exited the stairwell he heard someone shouting his name "Tyvon!" It was Michelle, and she was crying uncontrollably. Something was wrong.

"Shamel and Kane just got shot. Shamel's dead," she screamed hysterically. "I was talking to Shamel, and a guy jumped out a car, and just started shooting."

Tyvon stared at Michelle for a split second letting everything that she just said register in his brain, then he took off running down the steps. When he exited the building, he noticed two separate crowds gathering several feet away from each other. He violently parted the crowd closest to him, and saw Shamel's lifeless body laying face down between two parked cars in a pool of his own blood. Tyvon froze in his tracks. He couldn't think or feel anything. The nightmare that everybody warned him about had become true. His friend was dead, and there was no bringing him back.

"Where's Kane?" Ty yelled to who ever would answer, already walking towards the other group of people that were standing a few cars away from where Shamel was laying. Kane was losing a lot of blood but he was still fully aware of his surroundings.

"Where's Sha?" Kane asked Ty, as he kneeled down besides him.

Ty didn't want to tell him that Shamel was dead in fear that it might upset him, and make his conditions worse.

"He's alright. What happened?" Ty asked, with tears in his eyes.

"Slim," Kane mumbled grabbing Ty's hand. Before he could say anything else, the police had arrived, and was telling everyone to move back. Then they started asking Kane a million and one questions, interfering with the paramedics that just pulled up, and was trying to rush Kane to the hospital.

"Who did it?" asked one of the homicide detectives continuously, not caring if he was slowing the work process of the paramedics.

"You're gonna die god Damn it, tell me who did it," asked another officer.

"It was three white boys, they tried to rob me, they all ran that way," Kane blurted out, pointing down the street, providing the officer with false information.

The detective immediately dispatched some patrol cars off in the area that Kane had pointed to, and told them to be on the look out for three male Caucasians, possibly Hispanics. When Kane heard the Detectives orders, he looked over at Ty with a smirk on his face, showing signs opposite of what he was really feeling. The burning in his stomach was intensifying by the second and he felt his self getting weak but he tried not to show any signs of pain.

"I'm alright," he said, trying to catch his breath, noticing the worried look on Ty's face. Lord! Please watch over him, he thought to himself, as he watched Ty staring at him, as he was being placed on a stretcher and carried into the ambulance. He knew that it was over. The paramedics could prolong his death but nobody could prolong his life. Kane felt himself slipping away. His whole life was now flashing before his eyes. Close family members and friends that had previously past away were standing by his side talking to him. Come on, it's beautiful here! We're all here! Don't be afraid, let go, Kane had fought his last fight and he made sure that he held on long enough not to die in front of Ty. We'll remain brothers forever, nothing can stop that! He thought as he closed his eyes and exhaled his last breath.

When the ambulance drove away, Ty rushed back over to Shamel. The police had already taped off the area and had begun taking pictures of Shamel's body. Tyvon stood at a distance in a daze, staring at his friend who lay on the ground motionless. Draining his soul into the streets. Just hours ago they had laughed together, and made plans about their futures, but now that was all gone. He would never hear Shamel's voice, or see him smile again. For the fifth time in less than two years, death had struck close to home. Living had became a dream, while death had emerged as its reality.

Jackie came running out of the building followed by Tiffany, Jahiem, A.B. and Man. They all rushed over to Ty.

"Come on Ty, lets get outta here," Jahiem said with tears running down his face. He couldn't believe that Shamel was dead. I should've come down stairs with him. This wouldn't have happened if I was here, he thought as he took another glance at his friend's body.

"Come on ya'll, lets go before five-o starts fucking with us," said Man, thinking about the two guns that he was carrying, and remembering how the homicide police took him in for questioning when Lil Tray was murdered.

Tyvon didn't respond. He continued to stare blankly at Shamel's body. Don't sweat it kid, I'll handle this. You got my word I'll handle this, Ty thought as somebody grabbed his hand. "Ty come on, its time to go," Tiffany said as she led him away.

A.B. and Man went to tell Shamel's mother what had happened, while Tiffany and Jahiem walked Tyvon home. They both knew how close Ty was to Shamel, and even though he wasn't openly displaying how he was feeling. His silence showed his pain. After arriving at Tyvon's house, Tiffany and Jahiem kept him company for an hour before they went home.

The evening's events had become mentally, and physically draining for Ty. After calling Kane's mother and finding out that she and Wendy were already on their way to the hospital, he called Maxine and told her what had happened. Maxine wanted to come over to keep him company, but he told her to stay home. He was tired and just wanted to lay down by himself.

Six o'clock the following morning, Ty was already knocking on Kane's door. Nobody was home. They must still be at the hospital, he thought as he got into the elevator. I'll come back in about an hour. They should all be back by then, he said to himself. Walking out of the building, he saw Kane's mother and father getting out of a car. Kane's mother was practically being carried by her husband. A cold chill ran up Ty's spine once she spoke.

"My baby's gone Ty. He's gone. They killed my baby!" she said crying, reaching out to embrace him.

This had to be a bad dream. Yeah! That's what it is. I'll wake up, and everything will be back to normal. Me and Shamel will be chillin with Max and Christine, and Kane will come over saying that we're whipped. Then we'll all go play some ball together like we always do. Yeah, that's what will happen. This has to be a dream.

As Tyvon continued to wrestle with reality, he began to reflect back on his child hood days that weren't so far behind him. Things had changed fast. It seemed just like yesterday when he and Kane met for the first time on the basketball courts behind his building. And it wasn't too much longer after that when they both had met Shemal. From that point on, they were all best friends, and everybody knew it. Thinking back on all of the good and bad times that they shared together, and realizing that they would never happen again. Ty broke down and started to cry.

"Its gonna be alright bady. Everything will be alright," said Mrs. Campbell, now controlling her emotions, and catering to Ty's. She knew that his love for her son was genuine, and that was very important to her. She watched both of them grow, and she loved Tyvon like he was her son.

"Come on up stair with us, so you can relax. I don't want you out here like this," said Mr. Campbell.

Tyvon fought to regain his composure, and wiped the tears from his face with his shirt.

"I'm alright" he said, fighting back his tears. "I have to take care of something for my mom, I'll come by later on."

"Okay now, you be safe out here," said Mrs. Campbell. "I don't want anything happening to you. Lord knows that my heart couldn't take it."

"I'll be alright."

Ty walked to the cab base, and took a cab to Maxine's house. His mind was racing, and it was hard for him to collect his thoughts. Everything that came to mind seemed to trigger off his memories of seeing Kane getting carried into the ambulance, and Shamel's dead body laying between the parked cars covered in blood. He constantly wished that he could some how rewind the hands of time, but he couldn't. The damage was done, and there wasn't anything that he could do to bring them back. He knew that the streets were watching, and everybody was probably already anticipating his next move, even Slim, so he had to be on point. The first move had been made, and the date was set. Now he had to respond quickly. There wouldn't be any turning back from this point on. So like Kane would say, he would have to finish the game. Right here is good, "Ty said to the cab driver, paying him, and getting out a few blocks away from Maxine's building. I have to call Danny, he thought as he walked up the street.

Be More Careful

Ced was in his burgundy Range Rover driving across the George Washington bridge. He had just come from getting his truck hand washed on 126 street and 7th ave, and now he was heading to his house in Hackensack New Jersey. He had just bought the house for his wife, trying to make up for all of the time that he was spending running the streets. And since his girl had been looking for a new apartment around the same time that he purchased his new house, he decided to kill two birds with on stone. When his wife moved out of their condo in Riverdale, he moved his girl right in. Times were good and everybody was happy. He couldn't ask for more.

Turning down the music, he checked the time on his Rolex, then picked up his car phone and dialed a number.

"Fam! What's up? Did ya'll do what I told ya'll to do with them burners?"

"No doubt."

"Alright. Don't forget to tell Stan to move the van to the garage on 145th street said Ced. "I'll get up with ya'll at the crib tonight at ten."

"Ced!"

Ced hung the phone up, turned the music back up and continued his drive home. Life was good.

Back across the bridge in the SoundView section of the Bronx, there was a double funeral being held. Terrence Barnwell and Kenneth Campbell were being laid to rest. A lot of people showed up to pay their respects. Even though Ty knew that Sahmel or

Kane didn't care for most of the people there. He could still feel the love and lost in the air. Wendy and Christine both sat up front with Ms. Barnwell and Mrs. Campbell. Tyvon stood in the back of the church watching everybody take turns viewing the bodies. He had only went up to view the bodies once during the hour that he was there, and that was all he needed. He couldn't take it. To him, both Kane and Shamel looked like they would awake from their sleep at any moment. Looking at them brought back memories of the many times that they had slept over at each other's house. Ty remembered waking up before them on early weekend mornings seeing the same peaceful looks on their faces that they had now. The only difference was that they wouldn't be waking up.

This was not a dream like he had wished, and seeing both of his closest friends lying in caskets surrounded by people and flowers made the reality of his lost set in. He was already feeling empty without them, and he wondered if that feeling would ever go away.

Kim and a couple of her girlfriends had just arrived, and they walked over to Tyvon before they went to pay their respects.

"How are you holding up?" asked Kim giving Ty a hug.

"I'm straight," he replied, "What's up with you?"

"I guess I'm alright. I mean, this type of shit is rough you know?" said Kim. "I'm gonna miss Kane a lot." She said with tears in her eyes.

"Me too, you know him and Sha were like brothers to me."

"Yeah I know," said Kim seeing that pain that Tyvon harbored for the lost of his best friends seeping thought his eyes. She couldn't help but to think back to that hot summer day in Harlem when she had told them that they needed to calm down. Now only four months later she was attending Kane's funeral. She hated funerals, and wanted to leave this one as soon as possible.

"Ty, let us go pay our respects," said Kim, "If I don't see you before we leave, give me a call, or come through my block.

"I'll get at you in a day or two," he said and the girls walked up the aisle.

After the service was over. Ty met with Maxine in front of the church, and they took a cab to her house. Maxine had stayed out side the church the entire ceremony, because she said that she wanted to remember both Kane and Shamel the way she had saw them last. Ty understood how she felt, and he respected her alot just for coming down there to support him and her sister. Especially her sister. Christine had been a mess ever since she heard about Shamel death. Her and Shamel had made so many plans for their expected child, and from the very first day they learned of her pregnancy. Shamel did his best to show her that he was going to be a responsible father, now he was gone. The love of her life was dead, and she was five and a half months pregnant with his child. That was more than enough for anybody to handle, and Ty knew that.

Just as Maxine put her key in the door, Tyvon's pager started to go off. It was Fat Danny paging him from Keisha's house. Ty had been trying to reach him since Kane and Shamel got killed. Soon as Maxine opened the door, Ty ran to the phone to call him back.

"What's up Keish? Put my man on the phone."

"He ain't here, but I just spoke to him, and he wanted me to call you," Keisha said then she paused, "Ty, we gotta talk."

"No problem, what's up?"

"I'm gonna call you back in ten minutes then I'll tell you where to meet me."

"Is everything alright?" asked Ty, sensing that something was wrong. Danny never had Keisha or anybody else meet with him for anything before.

"I'll talk to you when I see you."

An hour later Tyvon met with Keisha in the lobby of Harlem Hospital, and she explained exactly what was going on. Fat Danny and another person that she didn't know had got arrested in D.C., for selling an undercover DEA agent 15 kilos of cocaine. Danny was being held without bail, and he had Keisha running around trying to collect his money, so she could get him and his co-defendant lawyers.

This was a major lost for Ty. Danny wasn't only his cocaine connect, he was his friend and mentor. Everything negative that could possibly happen seemed to be happening all at one time, and Ty felt his whole world crumbling around him. Everybody that he looked up to was slowly but surely being erased out of the perfect picture that he had always' envisioned. His life had taken a sudden turn for the worse in just a matter of days.

"I'll bring you the money in the morning," said Ty and then he left.

The next few weeks dragged along slowly for Ty. After giving Keisha Danny's money and giving Christine all of Shamel's profit from their last buy, he was back to buying ounces from the Dominicans on Broadway. He had been trying to build his money back up so he was on the block 24-7, and him and Lite were selling everything themselves hand to hand. There was no longer any room for the luxury of having workers because his product was too low. The only person besides Lite he had money to pay was Barbara, and that was because her apartment was a necessity. Until he worked his way back up, or found a new supplier with good prices, he was back on the grind.

Early one morning after pulling an all nighter in his spot. Ty was suddenly awaking by Jahiem storming into the apartment.

"Get up nigga! It's time to handle our business."

"What the fuck are you talking about" asked Ty groggily.

"What do you mean what the fuck I 'm talking about? Slim mother fucker! What else?" Jahiem yelled making sure that he got his point across.

Tyvon immediately sat up from the couch and was at full attention. Slim hadn't been seen around the block since the night of the murders, but the word on the streets was that he had been hanging out with Ced and his crew in Harlem. Ty had already figured that one out right after Jackie told him the description of the van Slim got out of the night of the party.

"Where's he at?" asked Ty.

"My uncle just told me that he saw Slim go to Sharon's house late last night," said Jahiem, "And on my way over here I saw Ceds' Z parked on Lacombe and Commonwealth so I'm figuring he's still there."

Jahiem's uncle Tip Toe was the local crack head from the projects that had his hands into everything and always seemed to know everybody's business. If you did it, saw it, or said it, which ever one it was, you better believe if it happened, Tip Toe knew the whole story.

Ty had been waiting for this moment ever since Kane spoke Slims name, but all of a sudden he felt himself getting nervous, almost to the point of procrastination. He had never murdered anybody before, but it wasn't the killing part that bothered him, he had seen it too many times. What bothered him was the possibility of missing his target, or simply not completing the job. He knew that if Slim survived this attack, it would be on, and with him having access to a baller like Ced, with all of his resources, there would be no telling which way the beef would come at him next. This was a one shot deal, if he blew it, he knew he was as good as dead. Despite his fears, Tyvon planned on seizing the moment.

"Yo, you still got the master key to all the buildings?" he asked Jahiem, while checking the clip of his 45 caliber Ruger, then cocking it.

"No doubt," said Jahiem, taking the key off of his key ring and waving it in Tyvon's face.

"Give it to me," Tyvon demanded, hoping that what he was getting ready to try to pull off was going to work. "Check it, this is what I want you to do. Go get Tip Toe and tell him that I want to see him right now. After you do that, go wait for me in Lite's building.

"Ty don't leave me, word up," said Jahiem, he was eager to get in on the action.

Kane and Shamel were his friends as much as they were Tyvon, and Jahiem was ready to prove that.

"I'm not gonna leave you, just do what I asked and meet me in Lite's building, Damn!" Jahiem was too hyper, and Ty didn't think that it was wise to have him involved with what was about to happen anymore than he already was.

Tip Toe came to the apartment a few minutes after Jahiem left. Ty explained what he wanted him to do, and once Tip Toe agreed, they both left going their separate ways just like Tyvon told him. Tip Toe waited five minutes before he started making his way to Sharon's building. When he got to the building, he took the elevator to the 7th floor then crossed the roof to the connecting building and let Ty in giving him back his key in exchange for a plastic sneaker bag. Then he went back across the roof into Sharon's building, but before exiting out he stopped on the 5th floor and knocked on her door.

"Who is it?" a woman's voice yelled from behind the door after a few hard knocks.

I said, "who's at my door."

"It's me," Tip Toe responded standing in front of the peep hole as he could be seen.

"Who the hell is me?" the woman asked as she looked through the peephole to see who it was. "Tip Toe! What the hell do you want?" asked Sharon swinging the door open.

"Hey ma, what's up?" he said smiling, showing his gapped toothed smile. "I got some mix tapes and a car phone I'm trying to get rid of," said Tip Toe. "You my girl as I came to you first. Give me 100 dollars and its all yours." He said showing Sharon the bag in his hand.

Sharon was furious, "Tip, Toe, I know your crazy ass did not wake me up for no god damn car phone and some mix tapes," said Sharon, "Hey, you better get your ass the hell away from my door," she yelled slamming the door in his face.

Tip Toe then got into the elevator, took it two flights down and jammed the door so that the elevator was temporarily stuck. His work was done. That was the easiest 500$ dollars he made in a long time, and he was more than ready to reward himself for his work effort. The craving he had to start smoking the 100 bottles of crack that Ty had given him was too strong for him to even consider waiting any longer to get high, so he sat on the floor in the middle of the elevator and began to smoke.

The slamming of the door made Slim jump up out of his sleep. "What was that?" he asked grabbing for his gun that he had tucked under the pillow as Sharon entered back into the room.

"It isn't anything." She said, "That was just crack head ass Tip Toe trying to sell me a car phone and some mix tapes he probably just stole out of somebody car," said Sharon, getting back into the bed with Slim. "He got some nerve coming up here early in the morning. For some bull shit like that. That motherfuckers crazy!"

"Car phone and mix tapes?" asked Slim, curiously pulling Sharon closer to him and kissing her, when he suddenly realized that Tip Toe could have broken into Ced's car. Slim knew that Tip Toe was good for that type of shit. If the car was unfamiliar to him, it was fair game.

"Damn! He said to himself, now sitting up in the bed. "Did he tell you where he got the tapes and shit from?"

"No, and I didn't ask." Said Sharon trying to pull Slim back into bed.

"Let me go check on my ride first." Slim said pulling away from Sharon and rushing to put his clothes on. The last thing he wanted was for something to have happened to Ced's car while he was responsible for it. All he kept hearing in his mind was Ced telling him over and over not to drive his car over there in the first place. "If that nigga broke into my car that's his ass," Slim said walking out the door and pressing for the elevator.

He waited for a few minutes before deciding to take the stairs. "Their damn elevators are always fucked up!" He knew how quick Tip Toe was with getting rid of the things he stole so he had to move fast if he was gonna catch up to him. Just as he entered the stair case he noticed somebody crouched down in the corner of the stairwell. "What the fuck," Slim said reaching for his gun realizing who it was and what was about to happen, but it was to late.

Without any hesitation, Tyvon squeezed off five shots from his 45. Boom! Boom! Boom! Boom! Boom! So Slim tumbled backwards down the steps, Ty knew that he was definitely hit, but he had to make sure that the job was done, and before his departure, that's exactly what he did. He walked down the steps and stood directly over Slims body, and fired two more shots at point blank range into Slims head killing him instantly. At that moment an instant feeling of satisfaction and security flowed threw his veins. The adrenalin rush that he heard others talk about feeling after taking a life was now his own boost of energy and just like Shamel, Kane and everybody else like them, Ty enjoyed what he felt. Just like a person inhaling the powerful gray smoke out of a crack pipe for the first time, little did he know, he was already addicted to the feel of the kill. Satisfied with his work, he crossed back over the roof into the next building and calmly walked down the steps and out the front door.

A New Beginning

Word of Slims murders quickly become the talk of the town, and upon receiving the news Ced immediately called a meeting. As he paced back and forth, he tried to figure out who could have put this hit together.

"What's up with that young boy from Soundview that was running with Fat Danny? Wasn't them two cats that Slim knocked off his people?" Ced asked trying to cover all angles.

"You talking about little Ty," said Stan, "yeah, Slim told me that they all hung out together but he said that shorty wasn't a threat, Slim was more worried about Danny than Ty. For a minute he was thinking about hitting the both of them just to be on the safe side, but once Danny got locked up, he told me to forget about it."

"I don't think Ty had anything to do with it, said Rick, "Shit like this is way out of his league."

"So if it wasn't Ty, it had to be Big Paul," said Ced, taking a seat on the arm of the couch.

"Why is that?" ask Rick.

"Because it's too much of a fucking coincidence that a week after I tell him to either start buying his work from us, or shut down, Slim gets killed, That's why!"

"Yeah, I could fell that, because Paul is probably the only nigga over there stupid enough to think that he could get away with some shit like this, said Mel.

"Word up! He's definitely been getting in the way with all of his fake big nigga shit anyway," said Stan, "I told ya'll before that we was gonna have to bust a cap in his ass sooner or later, so why not take the opportunity to return his bitch ass to his sender now?"

"Say no more," said Ced ending the meeting.

Back in the Bronx Tyvon sat on the couch in his mother's living room with the phone on his lap waiting anxiously for it to ring. It wasn't 4 o'clock in the afternoon and he was expecting a call from his man Kenny from Forest Project. Ty had met Kenny through Kane about a year prior to his death and from their first encounter they immediately bonded. Kenny fit right in with the crew and everybody liked him because he was just like them. Every now and then, Ty would go with Kane to Forest Project to hang out with Kenny and his boys, or Kenny would go to Soundview to hang out with them.

After Kane and Shamel's wake, Kenny went to Soundview projects to try to persuade Ty into going out of town with him for awhile. Kenny had just got plugged into a coke block out in Baltimore and with all of the craziness going on. He thought that it would be a good idea for Ty to leave the city for awhile and for him to make a few dollars while he laid law. But Tyvon refused. At the time of Kenny's offer, Ty was still unaware of Fat Danny's arrest and since he was satisfied with what he had going in the project, he decided to stay put, but now it was a different story. Life had changed for him since last time they spoke Danny was locked down and he needed to make some money bad, because right now he was struggling. Plus with the whole Slim situation fresh in the air, a change of scenery would be his best move, at least until he heard how the streets were talking.

The phone rang, and before it could ring a second time, Ty had the receiver to his ear.

"Hello!"

"What's up Fam? You ready?"

"No doubt."

"Cool, meet me down stairs in ten minutes. Our train leaves in a hour."

"I'm leaving now."

"Later," said Kenny hanging up the phone. Ty picked up his bag that he had packed with his clothes and walked out the door.

They arrived in Baltimore at 8 o'clock that evening and an hour later they were in the stash house and Tyvon was getting introduced to the rest of the crew.

"What's up Fam!" Shawn said as he opened the door letting them into the apartment.

From the way Kenny had described Shawn, Ty knew exactly who he was as soon as he saw him.

"What's up?" This is my man Ty I was telling ya'll about," Kenny said introducing Ty to everybody in the house. He continued, "Ty this is Shawn, that's Marky, and that's Pop," he said pointing each person out as he went along. They all greeted Tyvon with a hand shake and hug. Kenny showed Ty where to put his bag and then they got straight down to business.

Shawn began explaining how their operation was ran, really just reconfirming everything that Kenny had told him on the way down there. Shawn also wanted to know what name Ty would be using if he got arrested, and he gave Ty an address to go with that name. After he was convinced that Ty was on the right track, they went to grab a bite to eat at Crazy Johns on Baltimore Street. Shawn drove Ty around west Baltimore for a few hours showing him different parts of the town. Then they ended the night going to a hotel with two exotic dancers that Shawn had waiting for him at club El Dorado. This was the best introduction that Ty had ever experienced since he started hustling. Off top, he could tell that him and Shawn were going to get along just fine. There was no doubt in his mind that he was going to be very happy with his new team.

Part II

"Good leaders don't think in terms of friends and enemies, they operate in a world of allies and opponents, knowing that anyone they encounter can be one or the other on any given day and some times both at the same time..."

Cash Rules Everything Around Me

In Jacobi Hospital on January 23, 1990 at 2:30 pm, Christine gave birth to a healthy 8 pound 6 once baby girl. She named her Cynthia. Mrs. Rivera, Maxine and Ms Barnwell were all present when Christine gave birth and they all were excited about the new addition to their family. While everybody celebrates, Christine shed tears at the first sight of her child. Maxnie couldn't tell if her sister's tears were from joy, or from the pain of pushing out a baby that big. Just thinking about the pain that Christine had to feel while giving birth made Maxine put any near future plans of pregnancy on hold.

An hour passed before a nurse came and told them that visiting hours were over. They all said their good byes and Mrs. Rivera told Christine that she would pick her and Cynthia up first thing in the morning. Just as Maxine went to walk out the door, Christine called her back into the room. With everyone else gone and with tears still running down her face, Christine grabbed both of Maxine's hands and looked directly into her eyes. "Remember what we talked about, I don't want this pain for you, I love Tyvon to death and you know that, but if he doesn't want to see the effects of his lifestyle then maybe its time you change your heart. You'll get over the pain of a break up, but this pain is forever," said Christine now looking down at her new born child.

It was at that moment that Maxine realized why her sister was crying. Christine's tears wasn't from the joy of having a beautiful new born baby girl, nor were they from the pain she endeared while giving birth, her pain and tears were from acknowledging that Cynthia would never know her father. A senseless street beef had stripped Cynthia of her right to be daddy's little girl. And knowing how much Maxine loved Tyvon, Christine knew that she had to do everything in her power to prevent her little sister from feeling her pain.

"I know Chris, I know," said Maxine hugging her sister and now shedding tears of her own.

Late that same evening in Soundview projects, Big Pual was just pulling into the parking lot in his new pearl white BMW m-5, Dre and the rest of his crew was already there waiting for him. They were all on their way to Bentleys, Tip Toe had just finished washing all of their cars like he did every weekend before they went out to party. Now with everybody there, it was time to roll.

"Big Casino!" Dre called out waving for Paul to come over to his car. Dre was on his car phone with some girls that they had met earlier that week, and he was trying to plan their moves for the night.

"Play boy, are you trying to get your freak on or what?" Dre asked Paul, covering the speaker on his phone.

"Who's that?" asked Paul getting into the passenger seat of Dre's 780 Volvo coupe.

"It's them bitches from Queens."

"Man, I know a lot of bitches from Queens," said Big Paul nonchalantly like he had no idea who Dre was talking about. Dre knew that Paul was frontin because they always acted like that with each other when it came to the females, both of them tried to act like one had more girls than the others.

"There you go, you know who I'm talking about, Kara and them from Queens."

"Oh! Alright," said Paul now showing interest. "You should've said that in the first place, what's good?"

"They're trying to get into something tonight," said Dre, "if we're with it, they'll wait for us at the club, so what' up my nigga, is it on or what?"

"Yeah we can swing something. Tell em we on our way," said Paul getting out of the car.

Dre finished up the conversation as Paul walked to his ride. Eight cars deep, with two people in each car, they pulled out of the parking lot in a single file with the pearl white M5 leading the way.

Back in Baltimore Tyvon was coming up fast. For the first time since he began hustling, he was really able to stack his chips. Money was coming faster than he could spend it, and such fluidness was an unknown feeling for him. He was used to selling a couple hundred nickel bottles a day, and saving about a thousand dollars a week after shopping, but now he was on a totally different level. He was making some real money.

Shawn had four blocks in Baltimore, two on the east side and two on the west. Pop and Marky managed the blocks on the east while Kenny and Tyvon managed the blocks on the west. Each of them had their own section to run, and they each made 30% off of the daily income in that section. As a unit they took in 130,000$ daily. Tyvon's block alone brought in 30,000$ in a twelve hour shift everyday, and with in a few short weeks that made him more money than he made during the whole year that he was dealing with Fat Danny. Despite Tyvon's recent financial success, Shawn advised him to keep things going back in New York just in case they were ever forced to shut down, he would have something to fall back on. Ty immediately took Shawn's advice and started making trips to the city every two weeks so he could collect money and re-up for Lite and Jahiem, who were now working together under his request. Money was coming in from all angles, and with Shawn's help Tyvon was learning how to really organize and run a drug operation.

Tyvon found himself looking up to Shawn sort of in the same way as he did Fat Danny. Danny and Shawn both were about getting money, but Shawn's out look on the game was a little deeper. Where Danny Concentrated on making money, Shawn's focus was on keeping what he had after it was made. Shawn's philosophy was, making money was easy, but maintaining the money that you made was not, Like Danny, Shawn also recognized Tyvon's eagerness to learn about the life that he decided to live, so just as a teacher would teach his fineness pupil, Shawn pointed out the flaws and virtues of hustling. Where Ty lived to be ghetto fabulous, Shawn did not, and he warned Tyvon about rushing to spend his money on cars and jewelry. Shawn would always tell Ty if he didn't have house money on the side of his re-up, he didn't have money for a new ride, and Ty absorbed his knowledge like sponge to water. Just a few months ago he would have spent his first 10 grand on a new car, but since Shawn was where he wanted to be, he followed his lead. Instead of dropping 10 grand on a new car like he wanted to do, Ty bought a used Volkswagen golf to get around in until his financial situation was secure.

Everything in Tyvon life was running smoothly except for one thing, his relationship with Maxine, out of no where her views on life had completely changed and she had some how developed a strong distaste for his current occupation.

They were now living together in the Baychester section of the Bronx, and to Maxine's disapproval, Ty was only coming home twice a month for a three day period each trip at the most. It didn't matter how much money Ty sent her weekly because she just wanted him home. Tyvon had continuously tried to explain that he was working to make a brighter future for the both of them but Maxine insisted if that was true he would come home and get a job.

There was no doubt in his mind that Maxine's recent change of attitude was a sign of her insecurity, and Ty hoped that she would get over it quickly because he was almost certain that it would lead to their separation if she didn't. Even though he didn't have any desires to end this relationship with Maxine, he was already unconsciously using their arguments as an excuse to explore other avenues. Over the past couple of months he had elevated his relation with Tiffany on every level and since Shawn's girl Crystal had been making the trip from New York to Baltimore every weekend, Ty had introduced her to Tiffany so they could start taking the trip together. Tiffany made sure she came to see Ty every week. The good situations in his life were finally seeming to outweigh the bad and Ty refused not to enjoy the moment.

One day Tyvon, Shawn and Kenny had spent a few hours together mall shopping. They always took a couple of hours out of their day to buy some new gear before they returned to New York. It was alright to wear the same Jeans and sweat hoods while they were out of town working, but once they were back in the city, that was unacceptable especially if you was supposed to be getting some chips. They all knew that so it wasn't a problem for them to trade in their low profile styles for more flamboyant ones as soon as they stepped foot off of the Am track into Penn station. They were sitting in the sneaker section of Charlie Rudolph's waiting for a sales rep when Tyvon asked Shawn about something that had been on his mind for the past few weeks.

"Yo! S, When you first came out here, did Crystal start buggin out?" Ty asked thinking about his most recent argument with Maxine.

"Be specific," said Shawn concentrating more on the sneaker that he was trying on than what Ty was asking him.

"You know, about you staying away from here. Shit like that."

"Oh hell yeah, you see she brings her ass out her every week," Shawn said smiling while standing up giving himself a once over in the mirror before sitting back down and trying on another pair of tennis shoes. "When they love you they're gonna miss you. That's natural."

"I'm not just talking about her missing you, I'm talking about her wanting you to stop hustling and to come home." said Ty, finally getting Shawn's full attention. Staring over at Ty like he was trying to read his mind, Shawn smirks and asked Ty what was wrong.

"Maxines been on some real other shit lately, I don't know what's up with her."

"What did she do?"

"Nothing really. She's just been telling me to get my shit together and come home," said Ty. "The other day she told me if I don't come home within a month, I'm not gonna have a home to come home to."

Shawn shook his head and waved his hand in disagreement to Maxine's threats.

"Ty, she's probably frontin. All them chicks start screaming that come home get a job shit when they see a nigga blowin up," said Kenny.

"Word up!" said Shawn, I'm telling you she probably just scared that you might bounce on her with one of these B-more broads. That's all. I bet if you was getting this money in New York everything would be straight because she could monitor your every move. But since she can't do that, all of a sudden hustling is a problem. But check this out, if you was home broke that would be a problem too."

Tyvon tried to say something but Shawn was on a roll and cut him off before he could speak.

"Crystal tried that same shit with me but once I started tossing her a few extra dollars and telling her that I loved her a couple more times each day, all that other shit was out the window," Shawn paused for a second as if he was in deep thought then he continued, "Our situations may seem similar but the individuals involved are different. If your girl is sincere about what she's asking you then you should really consider it because that's a sign of a good woman. But if she isn't sincere, and her thoughts are selfishly motivated because of her insecurities, you're in trouble because her wants and need will always come before yours as far as she's concerned. It all balls down to you knowing your girl"

When Shawn finally finished his speech Ty was convinced that he was handling his situation with Maxine correctly. Shawn was right, her complaints about him hustling were heard of until he started going to Baltimore. Before he left New York there wasn't a problem.

Maxine was his heart and he wanted to spend the rest of his life with her but he refused to let her hold him back from reaching his full potential in the game. It was his time to shine and he was ready to ball like the best of them. It was as simple as that.

Bentleys was still packed at 3 in the morning when Big Paul and Dre decided that it was time to head to the hotel. All of the moet that Paul had been drinking had him ready to get his freak on, and the way Kara's girlfriend Tanya had been grinding up against him on the dance floor the entire night had just made things worse.

"Yo! Lamar, we about to roll out with these broads," Paul said to his lieutenant. "get at me in the morning when you get up, I might need your wake up call."

"I got you, go do your thing," said Lamar, happy to see that Paul knew that he could rely on him.

"And yo, keep a eye on that little nigga Jahiem," Paul said, watching Jahiem follow a group of the girls towards the bar. "Make sure he gets home safe."

Jahiem had caught a ride with some guys from Monroe projects but he hooked up with Paul's crew as soon as he got in the club. The guys that he had come to the club with had already left and Paul doubted that Jahiem knew that they were gone.

"Don't sweat it, he'll be with me, go do your thing," said Lamar assuring Paul that Jahiem was alright in his hands.

"Cool," said Paul, feeling good that he had responsible people on his team such as Lamar. Paul followed Dre, Kara and Tanya out the door. A lot of people were hanging out in front of the club when they got outside. Cars was riding up and down the street in what appeared to be slow motion, creating long lines of traffic. Stepping out the club, Dre immediately noticed that this car was blocked in by an empty double parked Maxima.

"Come on now," Dre said to himself looking around "Who's car is that?" he asked a group of people that was standing around talking, When they all said that they didn't know who's car it was, Paul suggested that Dre go ask the bouncer that was working the door of the club.

"I'm gonna go get my ride while you go kick it with homeboy over there." Paul had parked around the corner and he was hoping that he would have everything cleared up by the time he got back to the front of the club. All he could think about was getting his freak on with Tanya and he didn't want to prolong his desire any longer. His man Black from Queens had already given him the scoop on how much of a beast she was in the bed room, and he was ready to find out about her skills first hand.

Paul glanced over at Tanya and flashed a devilish grin as she begun to suck on his fingers while they walked to his car. I'm gonna tear her little ass up, he thought to himself while making a mental note to pick up a little whip cream from a 24 hour store before they reached the hotel.

As Paul approached his car, he pulled his keys out of his pocket and pressed the number two button on his alarm and both front doors on the M5 popped open. Once he stepped into the street he noticed that his car was slightly leaning on the front left hand side.

"I can't believe this bullshit," Paul said when he saw that his front left tire was completely flat. He stared at the tire for a split second in disbelief then he leaned into his car to grab his phone.

He never saw the two men approaching from behind him wearing identical hocky mask and camouflage army fatigues. Tanya looked up and managed to scream just as the two men began to shoot. Tat! Tat! Tat! Tat! Tat! Paul tried to climb into the car but was held motionless as the bullets from the Tec-9 and Mac-11 tore into his back. Hearing bullets buy pass her head and with broken glass flying everywhere, Tanya closed her eyes and tried to squeeze her entire body into the space underneath the dash board. She never saw the gun men grab Paul by his legs and pull him completely out of the car. "This is for Slim motherfucker!" one of the gun men said before firing four final shots. After a few seconds of silence, Tanya realized that the killers were gone. Still shacking from her near death experience, she jumped out of the car screaming, running back towards the club. "Help! Somebody please help me! My friend just got shot."

The vibrating sound of Tyvon pager on top of the hotel night stand had once again awaken Tiffany out of her sleep. She didn't understand how he could sleep thought that irritating humming noise, because it was driving her crazy. Who ever was calling him, was deliberately trying to erase all the numbers in his beeper, because this was the third time she had gotten up to stop his pager from vibrating. She noticed that the same number had shown up each time but with a different series of numbers behind it. 515-9867-123, 515-9867-1234, 515-9867-12345. Only girls do shit like that Tiffany thought to herself, she memorized the number before waking Tyvon up to answer his pager.

"Ty!" She said nudging him lightly. He didn't move. "Ty get up. I think you have an important call." Tiffany said rocking him out of his sleep.

"Who called?" Ty asked still half sleep, misunderstanding what Tiffany had said.

"I don't know who's calling, but it must be important because they keep paging you. Do you want me to call back for you?" She asked knowing that he wouldn't let her call the number back, but she was hoping for one of two answers. Hopefully he would say no and make the call himself in front of her, that way she could tell if he was talking to another girl, or he would ignore the call completely and turn his pager off. If he did that, it was just as good because that meant what ever bitch was calling him wasn't as important as she was. He always called her right back no matter what time it was.

Tyvon grabbed his pager and looked at the number, Damn! He thought to himself it was Maxine. For a minute he thought about calling her back but he quickly changed his mind, Maxine had become too unpredictable lately and instead of this call being of any importance, it might just be one of her, "I'm calling to stress you the fuck out calls," so he wasn't taking any chances of her blowing his spot with Tiffany just because she wants to argue with him at 4 o'clock in the morning.

"This can wait til tomorrow," Ty said turning his pager off while placing it back on the night stand and laying back down.

This nigga ain't going nowhere! Tiffany thought to herself as she crawled on top of Tyvon, sucking and kissing on his chest, slowly make her way down past his navle looking forward to taking her best friend into her mouth when she got there.

Jahiem was sitting in Lamar's Acura legend coupe when he over heard Dre talking about what Tanya heard one of the hit men say before finishing Paul off and immediately his mind began to spin. He couldn't believe that Paul had been held responsible for what him and Tyvon had done, Jahiem had heard rumors about Paul being the person that had Slim murdered but since he knew for a fact that it wasn't true, he never thought anything of it. Besides, he figured that nobody in their right mind would try to go at Big Paul, but tonight his assumptions had been proven wrong. Dead wrong.

Paul had just been murdered and he wasn't dead because of his own actions, he was dead because the streets believed that he was responsible for a murder that he knew nothing about. Jahiem knew very well that belief on the streets was as good as fact to a Scientist. If it was believed that you had violated another persons, family, property, girl or whatever, that was enough for the accuser to justify the taken of your life.

Reflecting back on this ghetto low, Jahiem began to feel a surge of guilt brewing up inside of him. He felt like he was the person that had just pulled the trigger and murdered his friend His love and respect for Paul made him want to tell Dre what had really happened to Slim, maybe their crews could get together and move on Ced. But what if Dre holds us responsible for Paul's death and then decides to make a move on us? Jahiem thought to himself quickly dismissing his desire to confide in Dre or anybody else on this matter out side of his crew. "Let me use your horn again?" Jahiem asked Lamar. He had to get in touch with Tyvon as soon as possible. "Go ahead, but don't be long because I have to keep my line open. The only way of contacting Tyvon when he was out of town was by paging him and since Jahiem didn't have a number for Ty to call him back at that moment, he called Maxine again to see if she had heard from him yet.

Play Hard or Don't Play At All

Noticing that Tiffany was in the shower when he woke up Ty picked up the phone and dialed his house number.

"Hello."

"What's up boo?" Ty asked like he had just become aware that Maxine was trying to contact him.

Looking at the time on the VCR and realizing that 7 hours had passed since her last call to Tyvon, Maxine shook her head in disbelief.

"Why are you just calling me back?"

"My beeper was in my coat pocket and I," before Ty could finished his story Maxine cut him off.

"So it's money or some pussy that's making my calls unimportant? I'm a big girl, you can tell me."

Ty ignored her sarcasm and tried to get to the reason she had paged him as many times last night.

"Look, I'm not trying to argue with you, What's wrong?"

"What do you mean what's wrong? A lot of shit is wrong Ty!" She yelled. Tyvon saw where Maxine was trying to take their conversation and he wasn't trying to go there. He knew that their relationship was on the rocks but if that's what she wanted to talk about right now he didn't have the time.

"Did something happen last night?"

"Oh! I guess besides Big Paul getting murdered last night aint' nothing happen, you know, just another day in the life, you know how it goes," she said sarcastically.

Maxine's words caught Ty off gaurd.

"Big Paul got murdered," he said more to himself than asking Maxine the question, "Where at?"

"Does it fucking matter? The man is dead, you'll have to ask Jahiem about all that extra shit," said Maxine, "Oh, yeah, Jahiem wanted you to call him last night, he said that it was important but if you would've called me back, you would've know that."

"Why are you just telling me this?"

"I tried to tell you last night but you didn't call me back."

"What ever," said Tyvon, disgusted with Maxine's attitude.

"Yeah! What ever," responded Maxine, I'm done with this nigga's bullshit for real! She thought to herself.

Tyvon heard Tiffany getting out of the shower so he began to end the call.

"Listen, let me call Ja and I'll hit you back later so we can talk alright?"

Instead of getting a response he heard the dial tone.

Tyvon couldn't believe that Maxine had just hung the phone up on him. He wanted to call her back but he didn't want to risk talking to her with Tiffany in the room so he called Jahiem.

"Hello." Jahiem answered the phone on the first ring.

"What's going on?"

"About time you got back at me," said Jahiem, "I've been trying to reach you all night, Maxine didn't tell you?"

"Yo, what happened with Big Paul?" Tyvon asked avoiding any conversation about Maxine.

"Paul got laid down last night coming out of Bentleys, Shit is crazy out here. I'll put you up on the whole story when I see you," said Jahiem, "When are you coming back to the city?"

"I'm still here, I'm in Jersey right now," said Ty. I've been out here with Tiffany since I left you the other day. I was gonna head back to B-More tonight but I guess I'll have to put that on hold for now huh?"

"Hell yeah! We gotta kick it for real. Shit is about to get hectic and when I tell you everything that went down last night you'll know exactly where I'm coming from."

Tyvon could tell by the flow of the conversation that some how Jahiem was involved with what ever happen to Big Paul and if that was true, that meant that he too would eventually be dragged into what ever was going on.

"I'll meet you on the block in an hour. Before hanging up the phone Ty added, "Yo, if you see Max don't tell her I'm in town."

"You got it."

Ced met Stan at Emily's restaurant on 111th and Madison Avenue to eat lunch everyday. Together they would discuss business in private and today wasn't any different. They would usually arrive at the restaurant together but when ever they didn't, Ced was sure to be the first to show up out of the two. Today was one of those days.

Like usual, when ever Ced was by himself before entering the restaurant. He circled the block twice, then parked a block or two away from the restaurant. He then walked inside Emily's, going directly to the bathroom. Only after scanning the entire restaurant did he take a seat at his favorite table. No more then 10 minutes after he was seated Stan walked in the door. It was like clock work.

As Stan approached the table he smiled at the sight of Ced. He had received the call about Paul's murder right after it happen and from their previous talks about Paul, he knew that Ced had handled this hit personally.

"All work and no play makes Ced a dull boy huh?" Said Stan smiling as he sat down. Ced returned his smile and took a sip of water. He would give Stan the details about last night's event after they ate.

Pulling up on the corner of Rosedale and Randall, Tyvon immediately noticed the familiar look of lost and emptiness on the faces of everyone standing out side. Even if he wouldn't have heard that Paul had gotten killed last night. He would have still known that a murder had accrued because only death could cause such a stale atmosphere.

As Tyvon walked towards Lite's building he reflected back to that early morning of January 11th, 1988 when he first experienced that pain of losing some close friends. Three years had past, and several live had been lost since that day. So many things had changed; even his reaction to death was different. Thinking of this made Tyvon remember something that his grandmother would always tell people when ever she was trying to encourage them to put their problems behind them. She would say that time was the best narcotic for pain. And at this moment Ty wondered if it was time, or the recurring murder scenes that he had become so familiar with, that now made him numb to violence.

Despite arriving a half hour earlier than expected, when he got to Lite's house Jahiem was already there.

"You're not gonna believe this shit." Said Lite as Tyvon entered the apartment.

After hanging up the phone, Maxine laid in her bed trying to build up the courage to leave Tyvon for good. She loved him, but she refused to sit around and watch his life be consumed by the streets and all of its short comings. None of the money, clothes, or jewelry that she received from him was worth the broken heart that was sure to come when it was all over.

Thinking of her sister and all of the other mothers, girlfriends, and natives in the ghetto that could identify with her feared pain on a first hand basis brought tears to her eyes. Her thoughts made her reminisce about the beginning of her relationship with Tyvon. Everything was perfect back then, so pure, so right. Tyvon was her world and she molded her entire life around him. She even held off on going away to college for a whole year just so they could spend more time together. And when she finally decided to go back to school, instead of going to Howard University like she had always dreamed, she enrolled in the more convenient Monroe community College.

All of her decisions in life were now made to comfort her relationship with her man. There wasn't anything that she wouldn't do for Ty and he knew that but his selfishness wouldn't even allow him to consider her feelings when it came to their future.

Damn! Why can't he understand how much I love him? Doesn't he see that his future is mine? The questions that she asked herself made her realize that she loved Tyvon more than she loved herself and that's why she hated him right now.

Feeling frustrated and confused, Maxine buried her face in a pillow and wept, leaving Tyvon wouldn't be as easy as she thought.

Back in Shoundview projects, Ty sat on Lite's bed and listened to all the details about Big Paul's murder, After having the whole story he knew that Paul's death was a blessing in disguise. Unlike Jahiem, he didn't feel obligated to assist Dre or anybody else with any retaliatory plans that they might be putting together to go against Ced but he would make his self available because right now, in the heat of the moment, that would be a good business move.

If Dre accepted his help that would be good because they could start working together, but if he didn't, that would be his mistake because Ty was still going to handle his business and unfortunately Dre would be held responsible for his actions.

Ced had just displayed his loyalty to Slim by trying to avenge his death and even though he didn't know that he had killed the wrong person, he showed that he was a major threat to Ty's' existence as long as he lived. Therefore, he had to be dealt with.

"So, what are we gonna do?" asked Jahiem, "Ced is already a big problem, and now we might have a beef with Dre if he finds out what time it is with us," said Jahiem snapping Tyvon out of a moment of deep thought.

"Please! Dre ain't stupid," said Ty, "Paul was the muscle, Dre aint no gangster, He's a business man, so he's gonna do what's best for Dre, believe that." Both Jahiem and Lite gave each other looks of bewilderment.

"It's time to step our game up," said Ty, "I need ya'll to find out if anybody in Paul's crew needs some work. If they do, hit em off."

"Where are you going with this?" asked Jahiem.

"One persons tragedy is another persons opportunity," said Ty looking at the both of his friends.

"What's that suppose to mean?" asked Lite.

"That means that we're gonna put this whole block on lock," said Ty, Slipping his pager off of his belt to see who was beeping him. The number that appeared on his pager surprised him. It was Keisha, he hadn't spoken to her since the day that he gave her the money that he owed Danny. I wonder what this is about? He asked himself before picking up the phone to call her back.

Keisha's conversation with Tyvon was brief and direct. She told him that she had some good news for him and that she wanted him to meet her at her house within the next hour. Tyvon agreed. Keisha had just returned from visiting Danny and what he wanted her to do was clear. Danny had been incarcerated for almost two years now and Keisha was still having problems collecting some of the money on the streets owed to him. One person in particular, by the name of Rasta Tone owed over 100,000$ and it was obvious that paying Danny his money back while he was locked up was the last thing on his mind. He wouldn't even return Keisha's calls anymore. Danny knew that dead men don't pay owed money but he had something in mind that at worse would make him brake even and at best would put him back in the game and that's where Tyvon came in.

Tone had been giving Keisha all kind of stories about paying her when ever they would bump heads but yet the word on the streets was that he was now selling weight, so Danny had planned to kill two birds with one stone. It was simple. He would have Keisha ask Ty to hit Rasta Tone and if he agreed, in return Keisha would plug him directly into Danny's connect but Tyvon had to piece Danny off with ten grand off of every load. If Tyvon accepted the offer, this deal would work out good for all parties involved. Rasta Tone would be dead, Danny would get his money back plus some, and Tyvon would have a direct plug to a cocaine connect that wouldn't give him anything less than 10 bricks to begin with for nothing more than 15,500 $ a piece on consignment. If Tyvon was mentally prepared for what Danny was about to hand him everything should work out just fine.

The Plug

"When can we do it?" asked Tyvon accepting Keisha's proposal without having a second thought.

In Tyvon's mind everything was happening for a reason and Keisha's offer couldn't have come at a better time. Having a direct plug to a consistent flow of cocaine was exactly what he needed to put his plan to take over the drug trade in his projects in motion.

From the time that he spent in Baltimore, Tyvon had learned that the key to controlling any drug area is to monopolize it, and that was only possible when the person putting the monopoly together was respected and able to supply what ever was needed at a consistent rate, and at prices lower than ordinarily obtainable. Tyvon had no doubt in his mind that he would be in position to put everything he had in mind together as soon as Rasta Tone dropped.

"As soon as you like," said Keisha. "Here's his address."

"It's a wrap," said Ty looking at the address on the sheet of paper that Keisha handed him.

"Remember, we have to meet Danny's friend tomorrow at 6 in the morning so be ready," said Keisha, She trusted Ty and she knew that he wouldn't turn down her offer to take the hit so she had set up the meeting between him and the connect in advance.

"I'll be ready, and don't be surprised if I show up with some good news for you to take to my man," said Ty; convincing Keisha that Rasta Tones days on this earth were in deed very limited at most. Basically, Tone was already dead.

Also in Harlem, Stan was cruising up 8th avenue in his 3000 Mitsubishi trying to figure out his team's next power move. With Big Paul now out of the picture him and Ced was back to concentrating on expanding their drug operation into the Bronx. They needed a solid outlet that could handle large quantities of cocaine on a steady basis and cozy corner in Soundview generated too much money for them to over look.

Stan knew that Big Paul supplied most of the dealers doing anything worth noticing in the Soundview and Castle hill area as now with him dead there was a major void to be filled. Stan was from around the area and he went to school with most of the hustlers that worked on cozy but since he was known to be Ced's right hand man, it was going to take him a little longer to regain their trust. Putting a crew together that he would feel comfortable working with was going to take some time.

"It'll be a minute but I'll put something together." Stan said to himself as he turned off of 8th avenue and drove towards the 145th Street Bridge.

Back in the Bronx, after receiving a call from Tyvon, Lite didn't waste anytime meeting up with a few members of Big Paul's crew. Most of the guys that he talked to was still in shock about Paul's untimely death and while they gathered together trying to figure out the motive behind his killing, it was clear that they also wanted to know what, if anything, was in store for their crew. Could Dre take Paul's place? Did he know Paul's connect? If not, does he have access to someone else that could supply him with enough work for him to keep the team together? And last but not least, what were they going to do about Paul's murder These were the questions that they were asking each other.

This is gonna be easier than I expected, Lite thought to himself. He was amazed at how Tyvon was able to foresee the vulnerability within Paul's crew without actually having to observe their reactions to his murder. Providing them with some work and offering assistance with any retaliatory plans that they might be putting together to go against Ced was ingenious. Dre and everybody else in Paul's crew knew that all of the young killers from around the way were down with Tyvon. And since he had been going out of town, his whole team was noticeably making some real money. The streets even began to call them Money And Murder, and now they had coke to offer at good prices.

Running with Tyvon and Lite right now meant strength, and that was exactly what Dre was going to need to get him thought this crisis. It wasn't said but the message was clear. Either Dre agreed to bring the crews together and make everything easy for everybody, or he refused and risked getting ran off the block, The take over was in motion and Dre's future was in his own hands.

"Don't' worry about Dre," said Lamar, fully aware of what was going on and accepting it. "I'll have him call Ty tomorrow."

"That's what I'm taking about, said Lite handing Lamar a paper bag with 500 grams of coke inside, Tyvon had told Lite to give Lamar all of the unbottled cocaine that they had if he needed some work for his crew and that's exactly what Lite did.

"Tell Ty that I said good looking," said Lamar stuffing the bag into his jacket.

Leaving Keisha's house, Tyvon was hyped but focused. He knew that he would be picking up a few bricks in the morning so he had to get his mind right.

As he drove up Madison avenue with his thoughts on setting up a distribution net work that would guarantee him a fast turn over. He was already moving two keys a week on the break down between his spots in Soundview and Castle Hill projects, and he was certain that he would immediately boost that up to at least four keys per week simply by adding Big Paul's crew to his team, and by making the size of his crews bottles twice as big as the competition. Tyvon knew that he wasn't dealing with a two brick re-up anymore so he had to stop thinking like he was. He had been preparing for a opportunity like this to fall into his hands his whole life and he was more than ready to transfer his thoughts into actions. He knew what he had to do.

After taking another glance at the picture that Keisha provided him of Rasta Tone from a birthday party that she had a year ago in the Cotton Club. Ty pulled over to a pay phone on 124th street and 7th avenue to make two phone calls. The first call he made was to Maxine telling her that he would be home in a hour. She still sounded upset but Ty was confident that she would be happy to hear that he wasn't going back out of town any time soon. He would tell her that in person.

His second call was to Shawn. Tyvon had already told him earlier that he wouldn't be returning to Baltimore anytime soon but he assured Shawn that their business dealings was far from over. Ty knew that Shawn could assist him with moving some nice amounts of weight in, and out side of New York so their business relationship was more important to him now than ever. After a brief conversation, Shawn had agreed to meet with Tyvon as soon as he came back into town.

Sitting back in his car, Tyvon reached into his jacket packet and pulled out the picture of Rasta Tone again. Looking at it, all he could think about was meeting Danny's connect in the morning, and just how much his life would be changed in a few short hours.

Cozy Corner

"**D**amn! Why does homeboy move so early in the morning?" Tyvon asked Keisha as he looked at the clock on his dash board.

It was 5:45 in the morning. The sun wasn't even up yet but him and Keisha was sitting in his car, out in Queens, parked in a McDonald's parking lot off of Springfield Boulevard where Danny's friend was suppose to meet them in fifteen minutes.

"I know," said Keisha agreeing with Tyvon about being up so early. "But it's worth it," she said thinking about the money that her and Danny would be making off of this deal. "Plus this is how Danny has been doing business with him for years, so I guess this early stuff makes him comfortable."

Looking into the rearview mirror, Keisha spotted a old model Buick Le Sabell pull into the parking lot, "I think this is him," she said as the Buick parked. She was right.

Tyvon observantly watched the tall brown skinned Hispanic male get out of his car with a knap sack slung over his shoulder, walk nonchalantly across the parking lot.

"Good morning, Keisha," he said as he got into the back seat of Tyvon car. Keisha reciprocated his greetings while the man leaned over to kiss her on the cheek.

Then he focused his attention to Tyvon. "And you must be Ty?" he asked flashing a bright smile as if he had just found a long last relative. "I'm Juan Carlos"

Tyvon returned his smile and they shook hands.

"I've heard a lot of good things about you," said Juan staring at Tyvon intensely, Juan's glear appeared amicable on the surface but Tyvon was able to see past his façade. There was a message there, Juan's mouth was smiling but his eyes were not. It was obvious that he was a firm believer in the old theory, "The eyes never lie," because he was searching Tyvon's eyes for any sign of disloyalty that he could find.

Juan's' gaze didn't bother Tyvon at all. Ty knew that him and Juan were stranger to each other so he understood why Juan was trying to read him.

In the streets, a person's reputation for doing "good business: could be the vehicle to lead to the door of opportunity, or "Big Business", if that reputation fell upon the right ears. But once you reached that door, whether if you stepped through it, or not, was up to you. On this level of the game all men had to either sink or swim on their own merit, not their reputation, and that was the message that Tyvon was reading in Juan Carlos's eyes.

"There's 12 keys in here for you," Juan said to Ty, patting the knap sack with his hand. The smile on his face was now gone. "All I want is 15.5 a brick," he said, "With numbers like that here in New York on consignment, we shouldn't have any problems." Tyvon agreed, and Juan continued.

"The more coke you move, the lower my numbers will drop," said Juan. "We are family now Ty." He said with a stern look on his face. "As long as you take care of me, I will make sure that you have everything you want when you want it. Understand?"

Tyvon understood exactly what Juan was saying. With out a long conversation it was clear that they were exactly on the same page, Tyvon nodded his head in agreement.

"Since that's out of the way, why don't you let Keisha drive this back uptown for you while you take a ride with me," said Juan, his smile had returned, "I promise that I wont keep you from your business to long."

Juan Carlos's intentions were to get to know Tyvon a little better and Ty recognized that and considered it a blessing. Usually guys of Juan's caliber wanted to stay as far away as possible but Juan was different. He only dealt with a hand full of people directly as far as business was concerned so it was very important for him to know the hearts of the men in his company. Danny had recommended Tyvon to him and even though he respected Danny's judgment of character to the fullest, he couldn't over look the fact that Danny and Tyvon were two different people. Therefore, to avoid any future possibilities of unnecessarily losing hundreds of thousands of dollars, or maybe even millions from dealing with Tyvon, Juan knew that he had make sure that they had a solid business chemistry with each other.

Tyvon knew that Juan wanted to use this time to get to know him but he didn't want to appear irresponsible, nor did he really feel like socializing when there was business to be taken care of. But a quick glance and nod from Keisha made him understand that turning down Juan's offer to hang out wouldn't be in his best interest so he agreed.

"I think we're gonna really enjoy each other's company," said Juan.

Despite his obvious concerns, Juan felt good vibes coming from Ty. And to him, good vibes always meant good business, and good business meant more money.

Later on that same day back in the Bronx, Dre sat at his kitchen table in awe as he listened to Lamar explain Tyvon & Lite's proposition. This was a bold move on Tyvon's part, but it didn't surprise Dre at all. Tyvon was always condully ambitious. Dre saw this coming months ago, and when he tried to point out to Paul how fast Ty's crew was coming up, and how much they had spread out, Paul told him not to worry about them.

In Paul's eyes they were just some reckless kids making a couple of dollars, but they didn't have a steady cocaine pipe line, nor were they organized enough to become real competition that could threaten his daily income, so he basically ignored them. Now only a few days after Paul's demise, the same people that Dre was told to over look was silently, but boldly giving him an ultimatum.

"I spent more money last night than these kids made since they started hustling." Dre said flippantly. "Are you sure this is a good move for us?" he asked Lamar.

"Unless you're ready to go to war with Ced and Tyvon at the same time, its our only move," said Lamar knowing that Dre wouldn't see a benefit in going to war with Ty right now when they could be uniting the block and making money together.

"Is everybody with it?" asked Dre

"I spoke to our whole team and they're all feeling this move," said Lamar, "Plus you know that most of the young boys that's down with us hang out with Lite and them anyway," he said. "The only difference now is that we'll all be getting some paper together."

It was like a game of chest and right now Tyvon was proving to be more calculated than reckless. Dre's focus was on keeping his team together, and most of all, on getting back at Ced for killing Paul and after listening to Lamar, he realized that the easiest way to accomplish that was to get down with Tyvon. The tides had changed and the strength now rested with the youth.

"Alright then, I'll give Ty a call tonight," said Dre. "Tell everybody it's a go."

Juan Carlos and Tyvon reached Keisah's house about noon. They had hit it off good. Tyvon was sure that he had eased any concerns that Juan might have had during their time together, so now it was time to take care of business. He said his good byes and headed straight to the Bronx.

Before leaving Keisha's house he called Lite and told him to pick Jahiem up and for them to meet him at Barbara's house.

Within 15 minutes of his call he was walking into Barbara's apartment. Lite and Jahiem were already there; Tyvon went right into explaining his plans for how he was going to divide the coke up.

"I never saw that much yea in my life," said Jahiem as he watched Tyvon take the kilos out of a bag placing them onto the coffee table.

"Word up!" said Lite in agreement. "That's some Scareface shit right there!" he said excitedly. Tyvon had told him that he was getting plugged in to a new connect but he didn't expect Ty to get loaded up like this on their first encounter.

"Yeah! Playboy, its on and popping," said Tyvon rubbing his hands together, while looking just as excited as both of his friends. "And this is only the beginning," he said, thinking about what Juan Carlos had told him earlier. The more Coke you move, the lower my numbers will drop...Tyvon knew exactly how to make that happen.

"Listen! This is what's going on," said Tyvon as he began to put the kilos into separate piles, "I just ran into Dre down stairs, we talked and everything is all good. Starting tomorrow all of us will up grade our bottles making them twice the size of everybody else, and we'll all use black tops," he said looking at both Jahiem and Lite making sure that he was understood. "After tomorrow, anybody out side of our crew that's caught with the same color tops as us will be dealt with immediately. "Tyvon looked around at Barbara standing in the door way trying to get his attention. He waved her off and continued. "Lite I want you to have A.B. and Man get the word out to everybody about this so that there won't be any excuses.

"No problem!" said Lite shaking his head in agreement.

"Also, Dre will be coming up here in about ten minutes," said Ty. "He's gonna give you 72,000$ for 4 bricks. Take care of that, and give him a extra 4 on the arm."

"Why we giving that nigga 8 bricks if he's only paying for four?" asked Lite candidly showing that he disapproved of Tyvon's' decision. He was already calculating his profit from handling such a load and now Ty was gonna give Dre most of their work.

"Because that's what I want to do," responded Ty. "Is there a problem?"

"Nah! It ain't a problem," said Lite. "I just figured that you would feed our team before you fed them other niggas."

"What the fuck are you talking about man?" asked Tyvon. That is our team now and this is what I want done, alright?"

"It's all good, said Lite. "You know how I am, it ain't about nothing," he said easing the tension that he felt building between him and Tyvon about the subject. He knew that Ty was going to do what he wanted to anyway so he decided to drop the issue for now.

"Alright then," said Ty. Check it, have Barbara cook the other four bricks," he said. "She usually gets a half a point over off of each key so we should have 6 bricks when she's done. Give her two hundred dollars and 150 grams for her work and bottle up the rest. I don't want nothing less then 40,000$ a brick," said Ty. "Do you think you can handle that?" he asked Lite.

"No doubt!"

"My man!" said Ty smiling and winking at Lite. "I have to take care of a few things, so I'll be running around a lot," he said. "I'm gonna need you to be on top of things for me."

"I got you kid," said Lite.

Being that Tyvon already had the coke in his possession, he felt an overwhelming desire to fulfill his end of the deal that he had with Danny as soon as possible. Reaching into his pocket, Ty pulled out Rasta Tones picture and address, and looked at it again.

"Yo! Come take a ride with me," Tyvon said as he walked towards the door. Jahiem got up to follow. "You right?" Ty asked Jahiem as he opened the door.

"You know it," said Jahiem lifting his shirt flushing the handle of the Glock that he had on his waist as they walked out the door.

As Maxine vacuumed the carpet in the living room of her and Tyvon's apartment, her thoughts were solely on Ty's sudden change of behavior. Yes, he was still hanging out a lots but she was very impressed with his decision to stop going out of town for her like she asked. To her, that showed that he really did care about their relationship and that he was willing to do whatever it took to make it work. She already had Ty back in New York, now all she had to do was convince him into getting a Job and leaving the streets alone completely. That would be her hardest task of all, but she felt confident that she would be able to make her plan work eventually. After all, Tyvon did love her; she knew that because he just proved how important their future was to him when he put her above his business.

Just a few weeks ago, the way he was acting, she would've thought that to be impossible but it was done. "I love that boy," she said to herself smiling as she picked his jacket up off the sofa and went to hang it up in the closet. Maxine loved her man and everything about him. Tyvon was her reason for breathing and she was going to make their relationship work for the best, even if it killed her.

A few hours later that night, Tyvon and Jahiem sat idle in a car across the street from Rasta Tone's house.

"Ty, we been out here for five hours man, are you sure this is the right address?" asked Jahiem with his gun in hand. He was ready to put his work in if he had to, but all of the waiting around made him feel like a sitting duck, and he was becoming very uncomfortable.

"Be easy," said Tyvon, Jahiem was asking too many questions, and he was getting on Ty's nerves. Tyvon was beginning to second guess his decision to bring Jahiem along with him instead of Man or Lite. "I should've left this nigga back in the Bronx," Ty thought to himself. Then he spotted Tones' Silver convertible BMW 325 pull into the block.

"This might be him kid, get ready," said Ty removing the towel that covered the UZI pistol that was laid across his lap.

The windows on the car were slightly tinted; all Ty could see were silhouettes. He was sure that it was two people in the car, a man and a woman, but he couldn't see any faces. He had to make sure that Tone was in the car before he moved.

"When the car pulls into the drive way, wait till his break lights go off then pull up," said Ty never taking his eyes off of the car coming slowly down the street. Jahiem was the driver and his job was to make sure that they got away quickly and safely. He was focused now more than he had been the whole night so all he did was shake his head in agreement to Ty's instructions.

As the BMW turned into the drive way, the street lights illuminated the interior of the car enough for Ty to identify Tone as the driver.

"That's him."

Just as the break lights went off on the B.M.W and the driver and passengers door swung open, Jahiem pulled up to the drive way and Tyvon jumped out the car firing. Tat! Tat! Tat! Tat! Tat! Tyvon had pounced onto the BMW so fast that neither Tone nor the woman in the car with him were able to react before he released the first burst of machine gun fire. Tat! Tat! Tat! Tat! Rasta Tones body jumped from side to side with the impact of each wave of bullets that hit him. The female in the car was knocked backwards out of her seat onto the driveway after receiving several slugs to the head and chest area. With in a blink of an eye, both Tone and his passenger were dead.

"Damn! Nigga, how many times did you hit that motherfucker?" asked Jahiem amazed at how calmly Tyvon sprayed the BMW and the two people inside of it with bullets. He had seen people get shot before but never anything like that.

"You know how we do," Ty said with a grin on his face. "For the right price, we'll kill a nigga twice," they both laughed and drove back to the Bronx.

Rasta Tone was officially history. Now it was time for Tyvon to put Cozy Corner back on the Million Dollar Map. In the months to follow, New York would be introduced to one of the youngest, most feared, Drug King Pins in the city's history.

Larger Than Life

During the next two years, Tyvon's drug operation soared past his own expectations. Not only did he accomplish the task of becoming one of the main cocaine suppliers in the Soundview and Castle Hill sections of the Bronx, but with Dre's help his organization had begun to spread through out the city into other boroughs. But that was only a minor part of his success.

The bulk of Tyvon's revenue came from out of town sells. Shawn had proved to be Tyvon biggest asset. With all of his out of state connections in places like, Baltimore, DC, Atlanta and Virginia, Shawn single handedly helped move between 20 and 30 kilos every week with ease. With Shawn and Dre on his team Tyvon had quickly became one of Juan Carlos' favorite people.

Just as he promised, once Tyvon started increasing his numbers of kilos that he picked up, Juan prices per key dropped significantly and that allowed Ty to share the wealth with his crew. Everybody was getting paid and it showed from the new house that Dre just bought in Yonkers, to the 30,000$ iced out presidential Rolex watches that they all sported, to six of the top guys in Tyvon's crew buying brand new Benz's in different colors all on the some day. They were doing it big and all of the competition was playing catch up. The game was on smash and the streets were talking.

"Who's loading him up?" Ced asked Stan. Tyvon's sudden rise in the game was on everybody's mind, especially Ced's. He had been trying to get a solid grip on the drug trade in Soundview and Castle Hill projects for

111

years, and after killing Big Paul, he was certain that he wouldn't be faced with any major competition, but his calculations were wrong.

To Ced, none of this made any sense, Paul was out of the picture, but yet his crew was clearly making more money than they were when he was alive and it appeared that Tyvon was solely responsible for their progress.

"I don't know who's hitting him," said Stan "But he's got it. I just spoke to my man from Lafayette, and he told me that Ty is passing them things off for 18,000$, and check this out, the coke is so raw, every brick you cook brings back at least 700 grams over without you trying to blow it up."

"Get the fuck outta here!"

"Word up!" replied Stan. "Boogie just picked up 6 bricks from them today."

"So Dre and Ty are partners now?" asked Ced.

"I think so," Stan responded. "From what I heard Dre handles most of the weight sells, while Ty's right hand man Lite handles the product that's being put on the block."

From What Ced was hearing he knew that Ty had to have a direct plug. His prices were too low to assume other wise. The average price per gram on the streets was 21$, Ty's numbers were 2 1/2 points below that. That was crazy.

Usually Ced would have access to enough coke to out hustle the competition, but for the very few times that he couldn't out hustle the competition, he out muscled it , Forcing other hustlers to join his team or to pay for their success wasn't anything new for him or his crew.

"I think its time we have a little talk with Tyvon," said Ced.

After Raseeda Placed the diamond studded name chain around Tiffany's neck they both stared at it excitedly as the diamonds' sparkled from the light in the mirrors.

"Girl! I am so not liking you right now," said Raseeda playfully.

"That shit right there is fly." Tiffany was speechless. All she could do was smile at her friend as she complimented her. The chain was beautiful. Tiffany's name was spelled out in script with diamond's covering every letter.

"How much do you think he paid for it?" asked Raseeda prying for information.

"I don't know and don't care," responded Tiffany. The price of the chain wasn't an issue for her. She was just happy that Tyvon didn't forget her birthday. Like she had thought. He had promised her that they would do something special this year for her birthday, but when he dropped her off last night and didn't mention any plans for the following day, she thought that he had forgotten his promise so she went into the house upset and tried to sleep her anger away.

It wasn't until he called her in the morning and told her to come outside to his car that she realized that his plans for them were far beyond anything that she could have expected.

"Alright! Whatever, forget the price," said Rasheeda waving her hand at Tiffany. "What time does ya'll flight leave?"

"Ty told me to be ready at six." On top of buying her the iced out gold chain, Ty was taking her to L.A for the weekend.

"Six?" Raseeda asked looking at the clock. "Girl, you better get off of your ass if you still want to pick up a few things from the Queens store."

"I know," said Tiffany. "We're leaving right now." She said grabbing her coach bag heading for the door. This was going to be the best birthday that she ever had.

Tyvon and Tiffany's red eye, flight left JFK airport at 11 pm and it arrived six hours later at LAX. Tyvon had booked reservations for them to stay at the Nikko hotel but despite how fascinated Tiffany was with the Luxury of their suite this was her first trip to L.A and she was ready to see the town.

"It's beautiful out here," Tiffany said falling back, arms in the air, letting her body collapse and bounce, lifelessly on the king size bed. "We're gonna put this baby to good use tonight." She said patting the bed, smiling mischievously.

"The bed is just for starters," Ty said with a devilish smile of his own forming on his face as he leaned over to kiss her. "Before we leave we're gonna bless their entire room."

"You promise" said Tiffany seductively licking Tyvon's lips and sucking on the tip of his tongue.

"I promise," said Ty returning her kiss passionately. "But you better stop fucking with me like this before we end up never leaving the room." Tiffany knew exactly how to get Ty hot. She also knew how to get him to respond how she wanted.

"Alright, I'll be good for now," she said biting Tyvon's bottom lip gently "Lets go get something to eat." Tiffany had been hearing about Rosco's Chicken & Waffles from her girlfriends for years now. Whenever they went to the Soul train awards they would eat there, and they always come back home talking about which celebrations they had seen come into the restaurant while they were there, and of course they bragged about how good the food was, so Tiffany suggested that they go there.

"It's your weekend," Tyvon assured her, "Whatever you want to do."

They both took showers, changed clothes, and after Tyvon made a couple of phone calls, they were off to begin their day. Rosco's was their first stop. Tiffany didn't see any famous faces while she was there besides the pictures on the wall, but that was a key because she wasn't the groupie type or the kind of person to be star stuck anyway. Plus like her girlfriends had said, the food was banging so she was satisfied with her experience. As she got her eat on she was startled by the sound of someone calling out Tyvon's name. "Tyvon!" When she turned to see who the voice had belonged to, she saw a tall brown skinned hispanic man standing in the door way waving Tyvon over to him. "Who's that?" she asked curiously, hoping that they would't be joined by any of Ty's friends.

"I'll be right back," Tyvon said immediately leaving the table to greet the man standing in the door way. It was Juan Carlos.

Back in New York, Dre was on his job. Just as it had been since their teams merged, whenever Tyvon was not around it was his responsibility to over see the daily operations. In Ty's absence everything ran through him and he loved it. Anything other than a position of authority with in the crew, he felt would've been degrading for a hustler of his stature. He explained this to Tyvon when they first talked about coming together and Ty agreed. From that day on Dre knew that there was a good chance that some of Tyvon's original crew, mainly Lite, might become jealous of the instant relationship and understanding that he had formed with Tyvon, and even though he knew that he had to monitor the situation carefully, he wasn't about to allow possible envy to affect how he did his job.

Just an hour ago he had gotten a call from Tyvon and before they hung up Ty told him, "To make sure that he walked the dogs tonight." Dre knew exactly what Ty was saying. Yeah, they did have two red nosed pit bulls that they kept in one of the apartments that they used, but the actual dogs weren't Tyvon's concern at that particular moment. Walking the dogs was a little code that they use that meant. "Get all of our money together." And that's exactly what Dre was doing. The coke man must be ready to drop off a load, Dre thought to himself as he ended the conversation with Tyvon.

Right now Dre was making sure that all of the money on the streets was collected, counted, and ready for the re-up.

"There's only 350,000$ here," said Dre looking at the money spread out on top of the kitchen table. He was clearly agitated.

"Nah man!" Lite refuted. "Are you sure? I know I had 400,000$ when I left the crib, count it again," he demanded.

"You just watched me count it twice, its only 350,000$ here," said Dre angrily. He felt like he was being played. "I'm not counting it again, it's 50 grand short." He said getting up from his seat at the table. "What's up with that?"

"Maybe I miscounted," Lite said with a bewildered look on his face. "I doubt it though. But just to make sure that everything is correct I'll take some shorts out of my pocket to straighten this out until we figure out what happened."

"Yeah, I think you should do that," said Dre shaking his head in disbelief. "Maybe I miscounted yeah right!" Dre thought to himself thinking of Lite's explanation for handing in short money. If this was the first time that it had happened he would be able to understand, but it wasn't. Handing in short money was becoming a habit for Lite, and each time, he so called "miscounted" it was when Dre was in charge. "I've heard it all before, Dre said to himself taking the money off of the table and putting it into a bag.

"50 grand is shorts, it ain't nothing!" said Lite walking out of the apartment.

Back in L.A., after talking to his friend in front of the restaurant for what seemed to be forever, Tyvon returned to their table minus his associate. Thank God! Tiffany thought to herself. She wanted them to spend this time alone.

"Boo, who was that?" she asked, happy that the man was gone but still wanting to know who he was because she had never saw him before. She thought that she had known most, if not all of Tyvon's close friends. That guy was clearly a friend. "Just a friend." Tyvon said nonchalantly with no further elaboration. Tiffany left it at that. She knew when not to push the issue.

When they left Rosco's, they began what turned out to be an all day shopping spree.

They went to the Fox Hill Mall, the Beverly Hill Center and of course Tiffany made it her business to stop at the Gucci store. She loved her some Gucci, and Tyvon knew that, so he allowed her to purchase everything from sun glasses to linen. She even picked up a couple silk robes, some house slippers and a few pajama sets for Ty which he ordered.

Never before in her life had she experienced this sort of financial freedom. With Tyvon no wasn't an answer, Whatever she wanted she got. He was spoiling her more and more each day. Life couldn't be better. Tiffany felt like a dream.

This was only their first day in Cali and just like she had expected before they left New York, this was indeed the best birthday gift that she had ever received. Tyvon was her king. And to show her appreciation she wanted to do something extreme for him, something so extreme that they both would remember how they felt for each other on this vacation for a life time. With this thought running through her mind they stopped at the tattoo parlor Cartoons before they headed back to the hotel. There Tiffany surprised Tyvon and got two tattoos. One of his name around her ring finger like a wedding band, and the other was of their names together drown inside of two connecting wedding bonds on her chest over her heart. Her message was clear. She wanted Tyvon to know that she wanted him to be apart of her life forever, and she was going to advertise that to the world.

The tattoos right now, and we'll begin working on our family as soon as we get back to the hotel, Tiffany thought to herself as the ink socked into her beautiful bronze skin.

Saturday might in New York, the last session at the Bronx famed roller skating rink, Skate Key, had just ended. The crowd was filing out into the street. Lines of cars drove up and down Allerton Avenue, while others were double parked blasting music, still entertaining the crowd. Lite was just one of the many ballers standing around enjoying his ghetto celebrity status as flocks of Skate key regulars walked by acknowledging him. This was a typical Saturday night for him, the only difference was that he was usually with a couple of his boys. Tonight he was alone, but that wouldn't be for long. The groupies were out in droves, so it was just a matter of where he was going, and who would be coming with him.

"Wus up Lite," two girls called out together both waving and smiling. It sounded like they practically had just sung his name.

"Bingo!" he said catching eye contact with the girls and waving them over to him. They moved with the kind of grace and unity that would bring him the gold medal for any countries Olympic synchronized swim team. Lite's wait was over. He liked what they were working with, and since he had hung out with them a few times before, he knew that they were exactly what he was looking for.

As Lite and the girls began to walk to his car, a powder blue MPV with dark tinted windows pulled up in the street beside them.

"There he go," said Stan.

"Let's holla at him," Ced replied.

The following evening, Tiffany stood frozen, eyes wide, hands over her mouth, clearly in shock when she entered L.A's legendary house of Blues and saw all of her friends as they yelled, "Surprise!" She couldn't believe it. First the chain, then the trip to California, and now a birthday party. This was the best year of her life.

Through Juan Carlos, Tyvon was able to put together a star studded but exclusive surprise party for Tiffany. All of her girlfriends had flown in from New York and celebrities from Shaq to Tyra Banks and P. Diddy were all on the scene, along with Biggie, Pac, Suge Knight, Tyson Beckford, James Prince and an up and coming rapper name Jay Z.

Kid Capri djayed, and Mary J. Blige performed, both tearing down the house. Champagne was flowing and everybody in the spot was on their feet getting their dance on. Not only was this the best party that Tiffany ever had in her name, this was the best party of the year.

A few hours earlier that same day back in New York, Dre was pulling up in front of a building in the Parkchester section of the Bronx. "I told this nigga to be down stair," said Dre to himself picking up his cell phone dialing Lite's number. Dre still hadn't collected the 50 grand that Lite owed and he wanted to get that done before he saw Tyvon tonight.

"Yo!" answered Lite picking up the phone on the first ring.

"You're playing games," said Dre "I'm down stair. What's up?" Once again Lite had managed to get under his skin.

"Calm down nigga! I'm coming down stairs right now," retorted Lite "Should I bring all of my clothes now?" asked Lite "What time does our flight leave? Is everybody else ready yet?" I can't believe this guy, Dre thought to himself. Lite knew that everybody in the crew that was going to Tiffany's party were all waiting for them at the garage. He also knew that their flight left in less than two hours so they were racing against time. "He's stalling!" thought Dre. "Look! Do you have the money or not?" Dre asked angrily. Before he could hear Lite's response, out of the corner of his eye he saw the nozzle of a gun pointing at him, entering through the driver's side window. Bloom! Bloom! Two shots were fired but Dre only heard the first one, and the last thing he saw was a bright light. "Damn!"

Game Over

"The past couple of years has been great for us, no?" asked Juan Carlos smiling lifting his champagne glass to toast Tyvon.

Their business and personal relationship had grown tremendously over the years. Prior to this event, Juan and his wife had Tyvon and Maxine stay with them at their mansion in New Port Beach for the Easter Holiday weekend.

They sailed on Juan's yacht, went to a couple of plays and ate at the most exquisite five star restaurants, all as a family. Something of that nature was unimaginable for Tyvon on their first encounter. Shit! When they first met, Ty was all but certain that Juan Carlos was going to have problems even trusting him. Their relation was put together strictly for business purposes solely. So to look back on that now, and to see how his relationship with Juan had evolved into true friendship over the years was special and sort of amazing for Tyvon to believe.

"Thanks Fam!" said Tyvon as he reciprocated the toast, surveying the crowd. All of his money, the condo's, the house, the cars, even this party, none of it could've been possible without Juan Carlos and Tyvon knew that.

"Yes! The past couple of years have been great for us," Tyvon said to himself thinking if Forbes had a Hood Rich list for Ghetto Superstars across the United States, I would have to be at the top." He smiled at the thought. The vibration of his cell phone broke him out of his Forbes richest men list day dream, but after answering his cell, he wished that it didn't.

"Don't do anything," said Ty. "I'll back in the city in the morning."

During the ride home from Kennedy airport, Tyvon's mind was working over time. How could I have allowed this to happen? It was the money that made me feel comfortable with myself about procrastinating to eliminate all potential threats when I would normally impulse... The money made me relax... It made me forget that on the streets cowboys are respected, while wonna be movie stars are preyed upon... It also made me forget that everyone is touchable in this game. I lost focus, and for that reason alone Dre is dead. "Damn, I fucked up!" Tyvon repeated to himself over and over as he reclined the passenger seat in Lite's Land Cruiser, listening to him describe in detail how Ced's crew had opened fire on him and Dre.

"Fam, it was crazy," said Lite dramatically. "I'm lucky to be alive."

Ty couldn't agree more. Losing Dre was a major set back, but if Lite would have been killed in that ambush, it would have been devastating. They had grown up together, and hustled with each other from the very beginning. Lite was down from day one, and after Kane and Shamel died, he had clearly emerged as Tyvon's partner and right hand man. They stuck it out together through the high and low points of the game, and once good fortunes become the norm, they shared the entire experience with each other. Basically, Tyvon viewed Lite as his brother from another mother, killing Dre was bad enough, but when Ced tried to kill Lite, he had committed suicide.

"Niggas think we're tender now huh? Tyvon asked himself out loud, angry but at the same time amused by the thought. "It's time to shake up the world Chico," said Ty, looking out the window at the other vehicles driving on the highway. Lite nodded his head in agreement, The Money! Murder! Machine! was back in motion.

Shawn Edwards had been sitting with his hands cuffed behind his back to a chair, under the bright lights in the interrogation room of the Bronx 43rd precinct for the past five hours. His hands were numb and swollen, and his shoulders were killing him.

"Come on Williams, I told ya'll everything I know already, you know my info is always good man," he said trying to stretch as much as he could. He was clearly in pain. "Williams, take these cuffs off man!

Agent Mcnally sat in the corner of the room silently, the tape recorder was recording, but he was still writing down everything he had just heard. From the beginning of the interrogation process he had down played his significance, leaving the stage to Detective Williams.

"Tip Toe, if you're blowing smoke up my ass you know what's gonna happen right?" asked Williams, hands firmly planted on the table that separated him from Tip Toe. "I will expose your ass," he said staring down on Tip Toe, burning a hole in his head.

"I'm not bullshitting you man!" said Tip Toe sweating profusively. He was already regretting his actions but he had just gotten caught red handed burglarizing a house. He figured, with his criminal record, if he didn't come up with some very useful information quick, he was guaranteed a first class ticket back to Sing Sing penitentiary for a long, unwanted vacation. Plus whenever he gave detective Williams top grade information in the past, not only was he released the same day, he was given a couple bags of Dope for his services. He had already missed his mandatory morning hit, and that was crucial for him to start his day on the right note. He needed his wake up hit right now and that was all that mattered.

"I told you, Tyvon killed Slim."

Four days later, while Dre's funeral services were being hold, Tyvon was experiencing the full reach of Juan

Carlos's connections. It had only been 24 hours since he asked for his assistance with tracking Ced, and Juan had already gotten a solid lead from some Italians he knew that owned a customized auto body shop in the Bronx.

"The car is there right now. He's scheduled to pick it up first thing tomorrow morning." Juan said into his cell phone with his normally deep but calm tone of voice "My people can take care of your problem," Juan said assuringly. Tyvon knew that having Juan's people put the work in for him, was probably the smartest thing for him to do, but this wasn't business. This was personal.

"Now, we'll take it from here, said Tyvon tossing his car keys to Jahiem, and motioning for him to get the crew ready to leave. "Good lookin, just let your people know that I'm coming. I'll call you tomorrow." He said flipping the mouth piece shut on his cell phone, ending the call.

Early the next morning, driving on the Bronx River Expressway, Stan and Ced were singing along with the Tupac song blasting out of the speakers in Stan's S600 Benz.

"I ain't got time for bitches, gotta keep my mind on my motherfuckin riches."

"That nigga Pac be spitting some straight gangster shit don't he?" Stan asked turning down the volume as the song was going off.

"Man listen, the shit he say is so real, I think he be talking about my life some times," Cedric said jokingly.

"Well, he damn sure wasn't' talking about your tricking ass in that song nigga,"

Stan responded, and they both started laughing.

Ced was know for openly spoiling any female he was involved with. The word on the street was, if a girl had a baby with Ced, he would put her in a nice crib and buy her a new whip." Ced was only 27 years old, and he already had seven children from six different women, and they all lived in nice apartments and drove new cars. His track record spoke for itself. He couldn't refute Stan's comments, nor did he try.

"We're the first ones here today," Stan said as he pulled into the open garage of the auto body shop. Normally it would be cars, SUV's and motorcycles, parked all over the side walk in front of the shop all waiting to be serviced in some kind of way. Today all of the vehicles were parked in the back lot.

"I like it like this." Cedric had never witnessed the shop this empty before, but he was alright with it because he preferred his privacy.

"They just better have my whip ready," he said exiting the car, looking around for his truck. It was nowhere in sight. "There better not be any excuses today."

"Better not be," Stan replied "Ain't nobody else here," he said while looking around to survey the scenery.

Inside the part of the garage that they were in, there was only a mechanic working. He was putting dark tint on the windows of a black Cadillac STS coupe. He was a regular.

"Mike, Wus up!" Ced said slapping the mechanic on the back. "Where's Bob?"

"Hey," Mike responded turning around to return Ceds greetings. "He is in his office, Go on in, he's waiting for you."

Ced looked into the office and saw Bob on the phone at his desk. Bob waved them in, then he held up his hand, suggesting that he could be right with them once he finished his conversation on the phone.

"Cedric, my man, Stan, what's going on?" said Bob hanging up the phone standing up to acknowledge them. He was always a little happier when a customer came to pick up a car because that meant that he would be getting paid.

"I hooked you up bro. Wait till you see my work. Nobody can fuck with me kid, Nobody!" he said loudly, full of animation.

They all laughed and followed Bob into the section of the shop where Ced's Range Rover was. As soon as they entered that area of the garage Ced immediately noticed the plastic on the floor. Every square inch of the floor was covered with plastic.

"What's the deal with all of the plastic?" Ced asked Bob, tapping Stan, taking his attention off of the other customized rides that he was checking out in the room. Before Bob could respond, Tyvon stepped out of the shadows, Mac11 in hand "That's to keep the stains off of the floor Ced" he said.

Jahiem and Lite emerged, pulling down the gates to the garage closing it off from the rest of the shop and the public. Man and A.B now stood in the door way that Stan and Ced had just entered, both of them with AK47 pointing at their targets. For a second the room was completely silent. Bob exited with out a word.

"What's this about?" asked Ced breaking the silence, maintaining his composure.

Ced spoke in a calm tone of voice but the change of his complexion spoke in volumes. He was furious. Everyone of these motherfuckers entire families are dead, he thought to himself. His mind was already focused on revenge, but Ced wasn't' stupid. Not at all. He knew that he had to be alive at best to bring his thoughts to reality, and at worst, his body had to at least be found for any of his people to have an idea of what happened. To Ced, all of the plastic on the floor spelled. "missing", so he hoped that he could play his cards right because if he didn't, it was a wrap.

Jahiem stepped up and hand cuffed Ced and Stan together by their wrist, then he made both of them sit on the floor.

"Where do you want me to start, Kane, Shamel, Big Paul, Dre." Tyvon said studying both men's facial expressions.

Tyvon was now sitting on a milk crate right in front of Ced, He arrogantly laid his gun on the trunk of the car besides them.

Listening to Tyvon run off the list of names made Ced's heart sink. He looked over at Stan who was now sweating and breathing heavy. From the look on Stan's face, Ced knew that his man was thinking that it was over for them. Ced had to think fast if they were going to get out of this one.

"Ty, Slim did that to Kane and Shamel, Stan said desperately, he felt his life slipping away so he was reaching for anything that might spare him.

"Big Paul owed me some paper and he wasn't trying to pay up," said Ced, putting his spin on the situation, hoping that Ty could respect the code of the streets, "What was I supposed to do. I admit that that was my work, but I didn't touch Dre."

"Word up. I don't know who put that out there," said Stan regaining his composure "Niggas just want to see something happen, that's all."

"Don't feed into that shit Ty," said Ced, seeing the bewildered look on Tyvon's face when he heard that they hadn't killed Dre.

Maybe there was a gap of hope. They didn't have any thing to do with Dre's murder and because his death was so recent it was obviously what caused Ty and his boys to react. The other guys mentioned had been dead for awhile now.

"Stop frontin motherfucker! That was me in the car when you rolled," Lite said interjecting. "I saw both of ya'll as clear as day so don't give us the bullshit." He said putting the nose of his Glock 45 up against Ced's forehead.

Now it was clear. Lite was the culprit. He set this whole shit up. The motherfucker was lying through his teeth and putting on a Emmy award winning performance to go along with his story. I bet Lite killed Dre. But why frame us? Ced thought to himself. Him and Stan had just hollered at Lite the night before Dre's death and they only spoke about a possible meeting with Ty to discuss some business. There wasn't any pressure being applied, no deception involved in their actions, nor was their intent to begin a business relationship malicious. They had already come to the conclusion that it was in their best interest to try to work with Tyvon directly, rather than war with him. Tyvon's team was strong and respected. He's number per kilo was so low that they were beneficial to all that could get in with him. Being the opposition at this point of the game wasn't worth it. The risk out weighed the rewards. It didn't make any sense.

After gathering his thoughts, Ced knew that it was over for them. Even if Ty had a change of heart, Lite wasn't letting them leave this room alive. His future depended on them dying today. Right now. "Ty I bet you, your man Lite knows more about Dre's death than he's telling ya'll" said Ced, trying to see the tactics of divide and conquer. Stan caught on and jumped right in.

"If we did what he's saying, we respect ya'll gangster enough not to be riding around with out burners on us," said Stan "We didn't have anything to do with that. Word."

"They're fucking lying," said Lite. "Ya'll mother-fuckers tried to kill me."

Tyvon was taking in everything he was hearing. His whole crew knew about the conflict that Lite and Dre was having. Their power struggle wasn't a secret, but Ty couldn't find it in him to consider that Lite, his man, could be that devious when it came to family. Dre was a part of their team, the entire crew loved and respected him.

Crossing Dre was double crossing the family. Lite always kept their crew first. Naw, I ain't buying it. Ty thought to himself.

"Check this out," Ty said now pacing the room slowly. "Lite is my man, you're not," he said pointing at one then the other.

"But since ya'll are both trying to save ya'll asses by labeling him as a scum bag. I'm gonna give him the pleasure of killing the both of you."

"Fuck you!" said Ced full of anger, knowing these words would be his last.

"Lite, shoot these pieces of shit," Tyvon said in his best scarface impression.

"One in the head a piece for thinking about it. One in the mouth a piece for talking about," said Lite as he pulled the trigger.

Just like that it was over. Four shots were fired at point blank range. Both men were hit twice in the head and died instantly.

"Wrap them up and put them in Ced's Range," said Tyvon. "Ya'll know what to do from here right?"

"Yeah!" said Man already rolling the bodies in plastic. "Drill air holes in the cans."

Both men were stuffed in their individual metal garbage cans with two 45 pound Olympic weight plates in each can. The tops were welded on tightly and by 2 AM that morning they were both at the bottom of the Hudson River. The range Rover had been burnt to a crisp and the S600 Benz was in a chap shop in Jamaica Queens. The game was over.

Three weeks following Cedric and Stan 's disappearance, Lite was cruising down 8th avenue in his pearl white BMW 850 Alpine, getting his glow on. He was living it up. By killing Dre he had managed to influence Tyvon to do something that he felt should have been done years before, and that was to erase Ced and his partners from the map completely. Because of him, that was done. They were all gone now and Lite was the master of his own destiny. He was back on top.

Lite had been working on this ever since Dre got down with them after Big Paul's death. He felt disrespected and cheated, when Ty immediately put Dre in a position of authority over him. I was down from day one. I help put this team together. Me! But as soon as we get a direct plug into a real cocaine and heroin pipe Line, Ty wants Dre to do my job. He's only with us for protection. Fuck Dre! Was how he felt. Lite didn't like that move one bit. He believed that the addition of Dre to the crew was like a cancer and since Ty refused to acknowledge that, it was his job to be the team's form of chemotherapy. And on top of all of that, Lite had begun to feel that Ty was becoming soft. He was becoming too Hollywood. All of the first class flights around the world, all of the back stage passes to concerts, the court side seats, and the weekends spent on yachts with Juan Carlos and his up scale friends, had dulled Tyvon's edge. Lite felt that Ty was losing it, but now that Dre was gone, he was back to his old self and Lite was back to running the crews daily operations. Everything ran thought him again and he planned to keep it that way.

Lite was on his way to pick his son up from his girls mothers house like he did most weekdays around 6 o'clock in the evening. But on this day when he pulled on to the street where his son's grandmother lived, the police were conducting a license check. "Damn!" he said immediately thinking about reversing out of the block, but looking in his rear view mirror he knew that was a dead issue. There were a line of cars stacked bumper to bumper behind him.

The cars cleared the road block smoothly. Some drivers were stopped and asked to show their licenses, while others were waved through uninterrupted. The New

York City police department had begun to make these random road blocks the norm after the new mayor was elected. He was a hard core former federal prosecutor who believed in convictions over justice, so there wasn't any surprise to the people of the inner city that once he was in office, these license checks were mainly if not only, conducted in the black and Latino areas of the city.

One of the police officers in the street waved the car in front of Lite through, then he held up his hand motioning for Lite to stop.

"License and registration," the cop ordered as Lite's car came to a stop. What's new, thought Lite to himself as he handed the officer the fake New Jersey license that he carried for identification. He hated the inconvenient of the road blocks. The police always managed to stop the car he was in during these so called random checks, driving while young and black in a new car is a motherfucker he thought to himself.

Once the officer had Lites identification in his hand, he knew that he had his man. To be positive of that, he took one more look at the photo on the license and matched it to the driver again. Before pushing the button on his walkie talkie and drawing his gun, within seconds there were FBI agents running out of buildings, they jumped out of parked cars, and out of cars in traffic, all with their guns drawn as well.

"Keep your hands where I can see them," said the officer who had checked Lites license. He was now holding a FBI badge in the hand opposite his gun. "Roger Williams, step out of the vehicle slowly. You're under arrest." As soon as Lite heard the cop say his government name, he knew he was in big trouble.

The End

"Keep them all in separate cells," ordered FBI agent Steven Mcnally. "I don't want them to see or even hear each other until after we weed out which one's are going to talk."

A massive simultaneous sweep had just been successfully conducted with the drug organization Money & Murder being the government's target. Twenty three out of the twenty four people on the indictment were already in custody. That would've been a great day's work if it wasn't for the fact that the person still being sort after was the most wanted, the most infamous, the gangs leader, Tyvon Riley.

That was extremely troubling for Agent Mcnally because he had done enough research on the group to know that Tyvon had the money and resources at his disposal to vanish if time allowed him to work. This son of a bitch isn't getting away, he thought.

"Colone, bring the girl in," Mcnally said.

The female in custody wasn't being charged with anything, but she was picked up driving one of Tyvon's cars, and since she hadn't asked for an attorney, Mcnally planned on trying to squeeze every bit of info out of her he could before they was forced by law to release her.

"Have a seat miss," Mcnally said amicably.

It was obvious that Tiffany was terrified, Mcnally caught on to that when she walked through the door. His whole game plan was to work her emotions. He wanted to send her on an emotional roller costar beginning with fear and ending with anger. But to make all of that possible, he first had to gain her trust. "Why are you cuffed?" he asked walking over to her. "Let me take these off."

"Thank you," Tiffany said, relieved that Mcnally had removed the handcuffs.

"Tiffany, you know why you're here right?" asked Mcnally, now sitting back at his desk, Hands folded together under his chin.

"No," she responded, tears beginning to run down her cheeks again.

"Tyvon, is the reason why you are here," Mcnally said watching her facial expression closely. He had her full attention. Now was the time for a little pressure.

"I don't believe that you have done anything wrong other than being involved with the wrong kind of guy. But that's not a crime," he said reassuringly.

Tiffany nodded her head in agreement, Mcnally continued.

"What is a crime is you withholding information from me that would lead to the arrest of a wanted man. Do you understand?"

"But I don't know anything," said Tiffany. Mcnally interjected.

"Listen, I'm trying to help you help yourself," he said with a little more bass in his voice. "Tyvon isn't any good. He's a drug dealer. A murderer. A liar. He doesn't care about anybody but himself. Do you really want to risk going to Jail for life trying to protect a guy like that?"

Tiffany didn't respond, she was in deep thought. Mcnally had her right where he wanted her. "Let me show you how much your man loves you," he said sliding a folder across his desk to her. "You think he loves you right? Open the folder then, go ahead!" Mcnally urged.

Tiffany opened the folder. It was full of surveillance pictures. Pictures of Tyvon and another female on what appeared to be a vacation in Mexico with another couple.

Tiffany immediately recognized the man in the picture with Tyvon as the same man that she saw in L.A. The two hispanic females in the picture with them were strangers to her. But seeing picture after picture of this girl kissing and hugging all over Tyvon made her furious. She felt betrayed. He said he loved me! He promised to spend the rest of his left with me! He said that I was the only one, she thought as she went through the photos. There was no way she was going to jail for protecting him when he was probably on the streets right now running around with that other chick. No way!

"She's not in here, you are," said Mcnally sensing that the pictures had hit a nerve. "Ty protects her," he said studying Tiffany's reaction carefully.

"Do you know this man?" asked Mcnally pointing at the picture.

"He came to see Tyvon when we were in L.A. for my birthday," she said with renewal energy. "I don't know his name though."

Agents Colone and Mcnally glanced at each other verity that their gamble was paying off. The only people in the picture that they had a positive identification on was Tyvon and Maxine. And they had just learned hours ago who Maxine was after debriefing Lite. Everyone else was a mystery, but Mcnally knew that the man in the picture with Tyvon was of great importance.

The Mexicans that provided the FBI and DEA with the surveillance photos only suspected that the man was a Peruvian Drug lord who was known as El Flyo. Or as we would say in English, The Flow. Mcnally believed that Tyvon was the key to El Flyo's capture.

"What else do you know?" asked Colone, Mcnally was writing in his pad. "That's not enough."

"Um, I know that Ty sells drug in Baltimore with a guy named Shawn," she said. "I use to travel out there with Shawn's girlfriend Crystal to go see them."

"Go ahead," Mcnally insisted, still writing.

"I have some of Ty's money in a safe deposit box," she said beginning to cry again. At that moment she looked down at the tattoo of Tyvon's name on her ring finger. She was already regretting her rushers. "That's all I know." Mcnally was satisfied.

"Alright here's the deal. You're gonna take us to the money then you're free to go," said Mcnally assuring her that her cooperation is what set her free.

The witness list was growing. Two down, Twenty three to go, Mcnally said to himself. This is too easy. By the time I'm done, Tyvon will be beggin to become a rat, he thought to himself as they exited the interrogation room on their way to confiscate Tyvon's money.

In a house in Miami Florida, over a speaker phone Juan Carlos was receiving the news about his new problems from a friend that he had on his pay roll inside the New York FBI office.

"It's very bad," the agent said. "They have pictures of the morenos with El Flyo, and this agent Mcnally has been pushing the connection between the two. He thinks one's arrest will lead to the others. I think that his philosophy should be taken very seriously," he said ending the call.

Juan was very concerned. The case in New York was basically local right now, but if the right dots were connected it could became an international catastrophe. A lot of good people would get caught up in the net that the federal government was trying to set. With situations like this, it was impossible to predict what the next man was going to do when his life was on the line. Juan knew that. He also knew that this problem had to be contained as much as possible before it got worse.

Twenty minutes, and one phone call later, Juan was boarding a private jet that was leaving the country.

Back in New York, at her job Maxine had just received a call from her mother telling her everything that was going on.

"The feds just raided Barbara's apartment, and they arrested a bunch of Ty's friends," said Mrs. Rivera sounding very concerned. "They're looking for Ty."

All of the air had been knocked out of Maxine like she had just been punched in the gut.

"I'll call you back ma," she said flatly, hanging up the phone.

Maxine didn't need to hear any more of the story to know that this was every bit as bad as she imagined it could be. If she had learned anything from growing up in the hood, she learned that the feds played for keeps. When they came to get you, it was because they already had you. They had already tapped enough phones, and flipped enough friends, and scripted enough stories for enemies to secure a sure conviction. Knowing this, her emotions were conflicted. She was angry at Tyvon for being so hard headed. When it came to the streets, he didn't listen to her warnings and now her nightmares were becoming her reality. On the other hand, she was scared. She loved Ty unconditionally, and it didn't matter if he was right or wrong, they were partners and she was going to hold him down to the fullest.

"Fucking Ty," she said to herself, walking over to a co workers desk to call her house.

"Some money my ass," Mcnally said to the Agent Colone in disbelief. "There's over 700 grand here."

Mcnally knew that whenever the government confiscated sums of money this large, it always put a major dent in the former owners pockets. He loved that. He hated knowing that this young black criminal was financially secure at the tender age of 20 yrs old, while he had been busting his ass for the government, living pay check to pay check, for over thirty years, that burnt him up.

Mcnally despised Tyvon in everyway possible but that wasn't an isolated issue. He hated all drug dealers. He just hated the ones' who made a lot of money a little more. The way he felt about Tyvon now was exactly how he felt about Big Paul before he was murdered. Other agents in the Bureau felt that he was allowing his personal emotions to consume him. But he didn't care. He still spent every day and every night working to bring his target down. He was so obsessed with that thought that he began to have dreams about Paul spending the rest of his life in a tiny cell.

And right when he was about to turn that dream into reality, Paul was gunned down. Mcnally was devastated. He thought all of the work he had done over the years was going down the drain until his surveillance team that was watching, Dre, stumbled onto Tyvon. This was like a breath of fresh air to him. He couldn't have been any luckier. The Money & Murder crew was unknown to him, but Paul's death had placed them right in his lap.

From that point on he refocused all of his energy and attention on Tyvon's organization. He gathered information from local police informants, and from drug dealers in other parts of the city who were trying to wiggle out of their own problems. From surveillance photos' to wire tapes, the evidence had piled up over the years. He felt that this case was strong enough to convict Tyvon's crew, but Tyvon himself had proved to be more elusive than the rest of the bunch.

Unlike the other members of his crew, Tyvon wasn't hanging around much anymore. As a mater of fact, sometimes he wouldn't be seen or heard from in weeks. And when he did pop back up, he always managed to shake any tail that was on him. But the biggest problem Tyvon created for Mcnally was he didn't talk business on the phone, and he never dealt with anybody outside of his immediate crew directly.

Mcnally was impressed with the discipline that Tyvon displayed but he knew that he would slip up sooner or later. They always did. All he had to do was he patient, and keep collecting evidence so when the time was right, he could deliver a case to the United States attorney's office that was air tight. He wanted to make sure that everybody on the indictment would be facing a life sentence.

But there was a change of plans, once his surveillance team witnessed Lite kill Dre. When that happened, all of the waiting went out of the window. Mcnally didn't want the whole Big Paul scenario to repeat itself so he was forced to move in.

"Do you think she'll testify?" asked Agent Colone knowing that most girls like Tiffany usually changed their minds after some thought.

"She has no choice now," said Mcnally "She was holding money, so either she continues to work with us, or I'll charge her ass with conspiracy." He said with a gleeful spark in his eye as they drove back to headquarters. All of his hard work was finally paying off.

Tyvon was at his house in Westchester County New York sleeping when Maxine called to inform him of all the chaos. The phone rang twice before it was picked up. When ever Tyvon was in his house he always let the caller speak first when he answered the phone.

"Get all of the money out the house, and I'll meet you." Maxine demanded. "Leave right now," she added before hanging up.

Ty knew exactly what "I'll meet you" meant and he was up and moving. There wasn't any mistaken the urgency in Maxine's voice. If there was ever a time to do exactly what she said, how she said, it was now. Paranoid and confused, he was running around the house frantically, gathering identification, and documents to the various properties he owned, when he noticed a news flash appear on the television, interrupting the regular program.

"What the fuck is going on?" he asked himself. A few seconds later he knew the answer to that question. His picture was now on the screen with the words" Wanted by FBI." Over it in big bold letters, "Oh shit!" he said running up the stairs to his bedroom. "They're gonna have to work for this," he said to himself as he grabbed the two 45 caliber automatics from under his pillow, searching through Maxine's closet, he was thinking about all of the people he knew doing life bids in the federal and state systems. He could hear them now, "You should've held court in the streets. This shit here aint' for nobody kid!" Ty knew that was right. Freedom, prison or death. The two negatives were stacked up against the positive. But that was the life he chose. Of course he didn't want to die or go to prison. Nobody about anything does. But he was prepared for it if it came to that. He was also prepared to disappear and to continue living beyond his means while doing so. He always said, "if the feds slipped up and gave him a head start, they might as well close the case because he was ghost."

"Get it," he said grabbing the biggest bag from Maxine's Louis Vuitton baggage collection, then he ran down the stairs to the guest bathroom where he sat on the floor and began to unload the 2.2 million dollars in cash out of the stash box that was built beneath the tub.

In less than two minutes later, Tyvon was on the high way in Maxine's 5 series BMW wagon headed to the Pocono Mountains in Pennsylvania. "Thank god for Maxine," he said, making his get away.

In the Southern district of New York old court house, Lite was being debriefed for the third straight day in a row by agents Mcnally and Colone. Both agents were blown away by the amount of information that he was able to provide. Lite personally knew and had dealt with all of the other known ballers throughout the city so he was able to fill in a lot of the gaps in the FBI and DEA's intelligence. He talked candidly about drug trafficking, selling weight, how the product was being put on the streets, and where. In full detail, Lite had broken down the Money & Murder organizational structure piece by piece. He told them everything from the meaning of their coded phrases to anybody in the projects that ever allowed a member of his former crew to use their apartment as refuge if he knew it, he remembered it and spoke about it.

All of Lite's information was priceless as far as the agents were concerned, but when he began to talk about murders that himself and other members of his crew had committed at the orders of Tyvon, he raised the bar even higher. Mcnally couldn't believe his ears. Informant's had told him stories about Money & Murder taking contract murders from other organizations, including both the Italian and Russian mafias, killing indiscriminately as long as the price was right. But he thought that was mainly street gossip because he only had evidence of them being behind two murders, the killing of Robert "Slim" Melrose and Andre "Dre" Ford. But after hearing Lite run down the list, the body count was now at twenty, and that was in the state of New York alone.

It was at that point, that Mcnally realized that Tyvon Riley wasn't only contaminating his community with the drugs that he flooded the streets with, he had also became, and produced serial killers.

"These kids made the Gotti crew look like choir boys." Said Mcnally. Colone nodded his head in agreement.

The news of the Feds snatching up the members of Money & Murder hit the ghetto internet fast and hard.

Everybody everywhere was talking about it. Where was Tyvon? How did he get away? If he's caught do you think he'll snitch? What's the price of reward for information leading to his capture? Some people applauded the arrest, while others despised it.

The federal sweep had affected all five boroughs. The arrests were plenty and anyone with close association with Money & Murder were all shook. Especially after hearing about Lite immediately becoming a government witness. That was the biggest part of the story, and the streets and the media spread the news like crazy. Even two of New York's prominent local new papers had Lite on their front page. One of the headlines read: Money & Murders second in command, Roger "Lite" Williams sings like a canary. The streets couldn't believe it. Over night, Lite went from being one of the most revered hustlers of his time to becoming one of the biggest rats in New York City history since Alpo. The damage that this one man would be responsible for would affect families for generations.

The Pocono mountains had became one of Maxine and Tyvon s favorite vacation spots. When ever they wanted to get away from the ghetto paparazzi and be alone, this is where they would go. During their first trip Maxine had fell in love with the area so much that she had secretly begun to save all of her money, and for Ty's 18th birthday she surprised him with the purchase of a Villa as his birthday gift from her. Tyvon loved it as much as she hoped he would. Maybe even more.

Over the years the Villa had became their clandestine love nest. They had spent plenty of weekends together up there enjoying each others company, relaxing and having wild passionate sex. Anytime together, alone, away from the city always managed to re energize their desire for each other so they always looked forward to the benefits of traveling. Especially to their home away from home.

On the day that Maxine gave Ty the villa they both vowed to keep its existence and location a secret from the world. They wouldn't tell any family members or friends about their get away. This would be their little bat cave; a place where they could escape, and didn't have to be bothered. Where they could revisit, and continue to create memories with each other. Maxine felt that Tyvon already shared the rest of his life and belongings with all of his friends, so this experience should be theirs and theirs alone, Tyvon agreed, and from that point on whenever either one of them felt like they needed to get away form the world they would simply repeat the words Maxine used the first time that Tyvon asked her to go with him to the Pocono's, "I'll meet you." And that said it all.

Looking at Maxine sleeping in their bed so peacefully made Tyvon think about how lucky he was to have her. It also made him realize how ungrateful and selfish he had been in the past when it came to their relationship.

For so many years he had always considered his relationship with her as a sure thing, but now as his entire world was crumbling around him, and seeing how easy it was for people he loved to betray and abandon him in the face of adversity. Tyvon finally began to understood Maxine's true value. She was priceless and he was disappointed in himself because it took a life shattering experience for him to realize that.

"Hopefully it's not too late for me to make thinks right," Ty thought to himself.

Despite all of the chaos going on, he was still very optimistic about their future together and that was for one reason in particular. He had just spoken to Juan Carlos for the first time since the feds had labeled him public enemy #1, and like a true friend indeed, Juan already had someone coming to take him and Maxine out of the country.

"She deserved better and I 'm gonna give it to her," he

promised himself.

In a ranch styled home in Costa Rica, flocked by a small army, sipping his marnes coffee, Juan Carlos sat content with the decisions that he had made over the past 72 hours. Tyvon's legal issues in America posed a grave threat to the orderly running of his drug operation everywhere, therefore it had to be eliminated as soon as possible.

Now reminiscing about all of the good times that Tyvon and Maxine had spent with his family over the years, for the first time in his career, Juan had briefly begun to question his sacrifice first policy. The same policy that had helped him stay out of law enforcements reach, and while doing so had practically launched him into an almost mythical type figure over the past decade. That said a lot about his relationship with Tyvon.

Juan Carlos liked Tyvon a lot and he had grown to trust him completely over the years but they were in a business where in certain circumstances, sometimes, good people and good things had to be sacrificed if one wished to continue to flourish in his trade. And his history had proved over and over again that when a person chose to over ride these rules by allowing their personal emotions to dictate their actions, the consequences were devastating. Juan knew that all too well and that's why his reservations about his security first motto were very brief at most.

Upon leaving the United States he had placed a call to one of his most proficient hit men in the country ordering the immediate killing of both Tyvon and Maxine's. And now that their location had been verified, Juan waited anxiously for the call confirming their demise.

Looking around the room, she was pleased to be in a place that she cherished, but she was there under circumstances that she despised. Now awake, Maxine had returned to living out her nightmare. As Tyvon paced the room visibly in deep thought, she watched him and began to reminisce.

They had been together for five long hard years now. Their relationship had been through a lot of ups and downs during that period of time, but they definitely shared more good times together than bad. Yeah they had their fights about the business Tyvon was conducting, and the stories she often heard about his dealing with other women had separated them many of times. But their break ups never lasted long. They had both learned early in their relationship that they would be happier together than apart, so they were always willing to work on their differences. How did we allow ourselves to get into this position? Maxine asked herself thinking back to their first encounter.

It seemed like yesterday when she and Christine were approached in front of their building by Tyvon and Shamel. Back then, Ty was known in the projects for always getting into trouble and for being a playa. So at first she kept her distance from him but that didn't last long. He was persistent and Maxine soon found out that she had a weakness for bad boys with nice smiles. Before long, Tyvon was coming to the back of the projects everyday to see her, and long conversations in front of her building led to numbers being exchanged, and the exchange of numbers led to long late night conversations on the phone, and that eventually led to them dating regularly. Soon they were known to all for being an item and from that point on they never looked back.

Those were much simpler times. Back then their only worries were about how they could spend more time together with out being bothered by their family or friends. But as soon as Kane and Shamel were killed, life began to change for them as a couple and for Tyvon as an individual. Maxine couldn't help but to immediately notice that Ty had emerged as the sole leader of his friends and with that inherited leadership role, he began to take full responsibility for the lives and deaths of anyone associated with him or his group.

Loyalty was a major part of Tyvon s personality when it came to his friends, but over night he had became loyal almost to a fault. It was like he had begun to believe that he had been born to protect and save the world, and if it cost him his life in the process of fulfilling his godly duties, then it was meant to be. Maxine hated that, because she knew that Ty's heart and actions were sincere, but she believed most of the people around him that candidly professed their love and loyalty to him on a daily basis, all had individual personal motive to do so. As long as he kept the money rolling in, and continued to make all of their problems his own, everybody would love him. They were all family. But if there ever was a turn in events, and it came a point in time when Ty needed those same exact people to sacrifice themselves for him in the same fashion as he did for them, the definitions of love and loyalty would be conveniently forgotten right along with their relationship with Tyvon. And that was exactly what was happening now.

A knock on the door brought Maxine out of her reverie and had Tyvon now standing with his back to the wall at the side of the door with twin Glocks in his hands. With the nod of his head, Ty motioned for Maxine to answer the door.

"Who is it?" she asked looking out the peephole at a short stocky, sterned face hispanic man that she had never seen before.

"It's Primo." The man responded. Maxine looked over at Ty shrugging her shoulder gesturing that she didn't recognize the man or his name.

Primo was the name of the person that Juan Carlos said would be coming to escort them out of the country, Tyvon nodded his head again, this time motioning to Maxine that it was alright for her to open the door. Entering the Villa Primo jumped right into his plan.

"We don't have much time to waste," he said scanning the room for any other occupants." Besides me, who else knows ya'll are here?"

"Nobody," said Ty.

"Good!" said Primo thinking the opposite. Juan wanted the bodies to be found immediately by the police, but he wanted that to occur due to regular investigation tactics such as tracing phone calls of relatives. No anonymous tips," Juan warned. He felt a call like that leading to the bodies would increase the FBI Investigation, putting more focus on him, and that wasn't the result he desired. Juan wanted it to appear as if the pressure from being on the FBI's most wanted list led Tyvon to commit a murder suicide pack with Maxine, and Primo knew exactly how to achieve that.

Killing them together as soon as he entered the Villa was his initial plan but after laying eyes on Maxine his plans had changed. Primo was mesmerized by her beauty. Her face, her bronze skin and perfectly proportioned figure captivated him to the point that he changed his mind and decided that he would kill them separately. Tyvon would go first so he could have a little fun with Maxine for awhile before ending her life as well.

"You won't be able to contact your families for sometime once we leave so I will allow you, Primo said pointing at Maxine, "To make a phone call from you car to let them know that ya'll are safe. You have two minutes." he said looking at his watch, "Bathroom please?" he asked

Tyvon pointed him in the direction.

Maxine had wanted to speak to her mother and sister ever since she left her office a few days ago. She knew that they had to be worried about her, and there was no telling when she would be able to talk to them again. So she jumped at the opportunity.

"Boo, hold up," said Tyvon stopping Maxine in her tracks. "Let Ma and Cris know that everything is going to be alright," he said convincingly. Maxine nodded her head in agreement then extended her hand. Tyvon knew what she wanted and he gave her one of the guns from off his waist. She put the gun in her pocket then exited the Villa.

In the bathroom, Primo was screwing a silencer on to the nose of a 9mm automatic. Thoughts of enjoying Maxine before killing her, already had him fully aroused. He knew once she was faced with the reality of her own death, she would do anything in her power to survive, and that meant to please him. He looked forward to being apart of everything, that she would be willing to do to extend her days on this earth.

After securing the silencer on to the muzzle of his gun, Primo waited to hear Maxine go out the door before he sprung into actions. Sliding out of the bathroom with the stealth of a cat and his gun drown, he caught Tyvon completely off guard.

"Don't fucking move," he said putting the tip of the silencer up against the back of Tyvon head, while relieving him of the Glock tucked in his waist band and tossing it on the couch.

"Dam, if this is about money, you can have it," said Ty thinking that Primo was double crossing him and Juan Carlos to steal his money. "Take it and bounce."

"Money. How much?" asked Primo intrigued at the mention of money. His orders were only to kill the couple. Juan never said anything about any money being involved. So if there was a few extra dollars to be made it was a bonus. Extra money plus Maxine was all a bonus.

"There's over 2 million dollars in the bag on the floor by the sofa," Ty said now rethinking his robbery theory. Primo was noticeably shocked when he mentioned the money, so Tyvon knew that this episode was more than a robbery attempt by a renegade employee. Tyvon had planned and participated in too many contract murders of his own for him not to recognized exactly what was taking place. For some reason Juan must have decided that he had became more trouble than he was worth so he had to be removed.

I never saw this one coming, Ty thought to himself. His entire life had just come full circle. The same person that had been responsible for his sudden rise in the game was now the director of his down fall. I always heard if you stayed true to the game, the game would stay true to you. Where is the loyalty now? Tyvon asked himself.

Now understanding that he had nothing to lose, Tyvon spun around with the speed and power of a professional football player, in result surprising his would be killer, knocking the gun out of his hand on to the floor. Without hesitating, Tyvon charged full speed ahead. But Primo recovered quickly, side stepping his lunge and landing a stiff left uppercut to Tyvon's body knocking him off balance. Out of pure determination, he was able to stay on his feet and tackle Primo. As they fell to the floor, Primo managed to grab hold of the gun concealed on his waist, and he fired three shots, Blap! Blap! Blap!, all hitting Ty in the stomach. Rolling Tyvon off of him, Primo got back on his feet and was now standing over Tyvon's limp body.

"You just had to make this difficult huh?" asked Primo, upset that he had to shoot Tyvon so many times, trying to make this appear as a murder suicide crime scene, now was complicated if not impossible.

"I was only going to shoot both of you once," he said rubbing the barrel of his gun on his temple. He was visibly frustrated, "now, after I fuck your girl, I have to beat her ass, then hang the bitch," he said pointing his gun at Tyvon's head to finish the job. Just as he pulled the trigger of his 380 automatic, the roar of the 45 caliber Glock that Maxine held with both hands echoed through out the Villa, Boom! Boom! Boom! Boom! Boom! Boom! Boom! The seven shots that she fired into Primo's body sent him spinning across the room into the wall where he slumped down to the floor. He was dead.

Dropping her gun on the floor, Maxine ran over to Tyvon. His stare was blank and he laid on his back motionless, spitting up globs of blood. Primos' last shot had struck him in the middle of his chest and his breathing was impaired.

"Come on boo, you ain't going out like this," Maxine said with tears running down her face, as she sat on the floor cradling Tyvon's body in her arms. "You're a trooper Ty! You better not leave me motherfucker." She screamed as she wiped blood off his face with her shirt. "Lord, please don't take him from me, please! She mumbled as she rocked back and forth, pressing his body tightly to hers.

Though her voice was now distant, he was still able to hear her every word. As Maxine prayed and urged him to hold on, Tyvon was being forced to accept the consequences of his lifestyle...Why should I die tonight? I asked myself this question as I lay on the cold concrete, Staring aimlessly in the air, not able to stand back on my feet... my body has been rattled with bullets, and I'm in shock feeling no pain; I am now labeled as another victim of society who has been trapped off by the game... Was this meant to be? Or will the lord save me? Why should I die tonight? And if I do, how will my friends react to my eternal sleep. Some people who once said they loved me, are now standing above me; I see some crying, some stare, while others act like they don't care. I hear ambulance sirens coming down the street, but it seems like they will never appear... My heart beat quickens and my breath becomes short, my mind races back over my life and I'm able to visualize my every thought... From my childhood to the present I dedicated my life to the streets; doing anything I had to do, so my money stacks would increase... But what did I accomplish? I never really lived; what happen to the fun family vacations, getting married and living in a house full of kids? If all fast money does is hurt, can someone please explain what is its worth? The average street kid wont' makes it out of his twenties before he is place in the dirt... It's sad that I realize this the day I might die.

But deep down inside I feel everything I did to get ahead was right, so unlike many others, my life wasn't a lie... my actions might have been wrong in the eyes of on lookers, but in my heart I felt what I did was right. And since this is part of the life I lived, I must let go, and accept why I should die tonight, he thought to himself before exhaling his last breath.

In death, the legend of Tyvon Riley had been solidified. Books and magazine articles were written about him and straight to DVD movies were made. He had been immortalized in rap songs, and people who had never been in the same room with him now proudly wave shirts with his likeness printed on them.

Gangsters and Hustlers everywhere, both young and old, reverently tell stories about his life. Everyone claimed to have known him, but very few actually knew the true moral of his story, or what he came to realize during the final moment of his life. The game had been true to him...

Once you choose the behavior, you chose and must accept the consequences, live by the trigga, die by the trigga.

The End

Preview of Next Novel

Written by Team Rollock

Say Good Bye To The Bad Guy: "A Gangsters Story"

Part 1

"Thoughts of a Successful Hustler"

My life is burden by the fact of an early end. 99% of the time I'm trying to out think the government, or trying to predict the betrayal of close friends:

Charlatans conceal envy, with only one thing on their mind; hoping that they will get their chance to shine, when it's my death or prison time:

Girls flock around me in groups; men surround me armed ready to shoot:

I can buy whatever is in a millionaires reach: even though I moved into a two million dollar home, I still crave to hang in the hood with my peeps;

I have a fear to drive through the city in the same car with my wife and son: because I would hate for them to be repaid for something that I had previously done:

But from the outside looking in, I appear to be living great:

I own a six car fleet, my family is beautiful, we have access to millions, living on a multi-million dollar estate:

But the reality of it all is, I wish I could start my life all over again;

I would keep my family, give back my money, and hopefully erase the envy out of the hearts of my friends:

I know this may sound like a joke; but my happiest memories come from the time when I was broke:

Don't get me wrong, there's nothing sweet about being poor; but before I had my Rolex, my Benz or my house, when a person displayed their love for me, I knew I was all that they saw:

My line of work has close friends working to turn me in while others conspire about my death;

And since the streets have already taken my freedom to enjoy my success, I often wonder what will it take next...

Chapter 1

"I just dropped the money off at the bails bondsman," Wop said into his cell phone as he reached out of the window of his new cranberry colored 911 turbo Porsche to fling a token into the toll machine on the Whitestone Bridge.

"I'm on my way to Rikers Island now," he said now checking the time on his diamond flooded Breitling watch. "I hope I'm not waiting in that parking lot all night for them to release his ass".

Wop knew that he was playing it close. His mother in-law was flying into town in a few hours and he had already promised his wife that he would be at the airport when she arrived. If for any reason he managed to have her waiting for him for a long period of time, or even worse, if some how he didn't show up at all, Nancy would never let him hear the end of it.

"I don't need this shit in my life," he said out loud, more to himself than to anyone else.

"Are you sure your alright with this?" asked Wops partner into the phone already knowing to answer to his question. "Because if not, I can handle it."

"Fuck it now, I'm already half way there," Wop said checking the time on his watch again.

"If worse comes to worse, I'll take him with me to the airport. Either way I'll be alright."

"Cool! I'm not going anywhere tonight so call me here later," the man said ending the call knowing that for Wop this situation in particular was more undesirable than the others. He also understood that true commitments were never easily honored. If they were, then everyone would be trustworthy and reliable. A lot of problems in the world would be non existent. But that was only in a dream world. This was real life, where real people had to make real decisions.

Wop was the epitome of a gangster so if there was anyone capable of pushing their emotions aside to go through with bailing a childhood friend out of jail solely to kill him, he was the man.

"This isn't anything new to him", he said to himself as he picked the remote up off of the marble coffee table and began to flip through the channels of the 60 inch flat T.V. hanging on his living room wall.

After the conversation with his partner, Wop tried to focus on the task in front of him like he normally did before he put in work, but today was different. His focus was lost. Usually he would put together a plan, then execute it efficiently but today his only plan was to improvise. The lack of preparation made him begin to question himself. Maybe being a boss, and all the years of giving orders to others for situations like this had dulled his killer instinct. Or was it something else distracting him? Wop pondered these thoughts as he drove in silence.

Murdering a friend was the last thing he wanted to have on his resume, but just like there was a price to pay for violating the rules of The Constellation, there was also a price to pay for being a loyal member of such an organization. Rules are rules, and they applied to everyone. He understood that clearly, what he didn't understand and recently had begun to question, was how something that was originally designed to keep everyone together was now tearing them all apart? The only law that seemed to exist as of late was, "Get them before they get you. Pull your gun first, shoot fast and when you kill, don't ever stop killing". Where there was supposed to be loyalty and honor weaved into a business relationship amongst friends, there was paranoia breeding deception. Somewhere down the line, over the years, the vision initially held had been lost. Did greed set in? Envy? Jealousy? Have we begun to care too much about our business ventures, and too little about each other as people? What misled us? Driving now in a dream like state, Wop began reflecting back on to how it all began.

Chapter II

Happy New Years! Everyone chanted in unison as the clock struck midnight. The year was 1993 and the Tavern on the Green, on Central Park in Manhattan was packed. People from all walks of life attended the posh new years celebration, but there was no mistaking that this gathering was a hustlers convention.

Everyone inside was some how apart of New York Cities elite atmosphere and it showed. For a day, the guys had traded in their uptowns, army jackets and jeans, for gators, full length minks, and tailor made suits. But the women, they stole the show adorned in high fashion garments such as Dior, Chanel, and Dolce & Gabbana. They all looked like they were movie stars ready to hit the red carpet for the Oscars.

The only thing missing was Star Jones asking, "who are you wearing ?" Everyone was dressed to impress, especially the young men sitting at the table with the legendary South Side Jamaica Queens drug Kingpin, Wayne Givens.

"Happy new years fellas," said Wayne lifting his wine glass giving a toast to everyone that had just brung in the new years with him.

"Happy new years," retorted Simon, Wop and Fame, all reciprocating Wayne's toast.

They had all been doing business together for years but since Wayne normally spent all major holidays with his wife and family, the guys were honored that he had invited them out with him tonight. Without a doubt a major statement was being made, but at first glance no one, not even the people sitting at the table knew exactly what was being said. But it wouldn't take them long to find out.

"This is a beautiful evening. All of you are looking sharp," Wayne said openly pleased with everyone's appearance at his table. It wasn't too long ago when the boys everyday attire would've consisted of hooded sweatshirts, army fatigues and Timberland boots. They had come a long way in a short period of time under Wayne's tutelage, and he was pleased with their achievements.

"And look at you," he said grabbing Simons arm, admiring the diamond faced Presidential Rolex that sparkled on his wrist. "You are just like your Dad."

That was the best thing he could have said to Simon. Not only was his farther his idol, he was also the man that taught Wayne everything he knew. Basically, if it hadn't been for Simon Barry Sr, Wayne would've probably been in prison or even dead by now, and that wasn't a secret.

Simon nodded his head in agreement and smiled at the compliments.

"I remember the day I got down with your Dad. This was back when he had 116th street and Manhattan Ave rocking. Dope fiends formed lines that went around the corner. Woo Wee!, "he exclaimed, enjoying every minute of his trip down memory lane.

The guys loved to hear Wayne's old school stories so they candidly displayed their interest so he would continue.

"We had that pure China White heroin, and that made our stamp Big Apple and Times up, worth millions. If you wasn't affiliated with our thang then you wasn't really making any money on the dope tip. We had the game locked down, clearing an easy 200 grand everyday. Now that was some real paper. A clean six month run made you a millionaire a few times over. And the thing that made your farther one of the most revered hustlers of his time was, he wasn't greedy," Wayne said now appearing to be bringing his thoughts and focus back into the present day and time.

"He made sure that all of us got rich and that's what I intend to do for ya'll," he said pausing briefly to refill everyone's glass with more champagne. "Fellas, I'm retired as of this very moment. Everything is in ya'll hands from now on."

When Wayne ended that last sentence, for a split second no words were spoken. Wop, Simon and Fame all glanced at each other clearly bemused. They couldn't believe what they just heard. Wop in particular didn't know if he should be happy and celebrate Wayne's retirement, or if he should be sad and loathe his mentors departure. Simon broke the silence.

"What are you talking about?" he asked with a sign of disbelief on his face. "You aint ready to leave all of this behind," Simon said gesturing to everyone and everything around them.

"I'm done," Wayne said with strong conviction. "My mind is made up. I'm almost 50 years old, I've been in the streets all my life and by the blessing of God I have never been to prison or better yet, even convicted of a crime. My health is good, my family is doing great. I have double digit millions tucked away, and with all of that in mind, I think that it is time for me to stop rolling the dice. I've beaten all of the odds so far, but I know that a person can only gamble with their life for so long before they crap out. I want to avoid the story book ending for a nigga like me. Ten years from now I don't want to be walking around the yard in Lewisburg talking about how I was doing it when I was in the town. I want to be traveling around the world still living large with the streets saying, "Wayne Givens was the best that ever did it and got away with it," so I'm getting out while I still have a chance," he said erasing any doubt about his proclaimed retirement.

This shit was real, Wop thought to himself. What were they suppose to do now? For the past five years Wayne had orchestrated their every move within the drug world, and because of his guidance they had experienced success beyond their years. Wayne had all the answers. But now what do we do? Fame and Simon have been my partners for years. Does this mean we'll all be going our own ways? Or will someone step up and be Boss?

Just as these thoughts rolled around in Wop's head, it was like Wayne was able to read his mind because he immediately began to lay out a plan of organization that he wanted them to follow.

"I know that this is a bit confusing because I didn't give you guys a heads up, but here's the deal. I want everything to continue to operate in balance exactly how they have been."

"How is that possible with you gone?" asked Wop. He was still trying to make sense out of all this.

"It's really simple, you will continue to be responsible for all sales and distribution of the crack. Simon will manage the heroin and Fame will still be in charge of all powder cocaine sales. Ya'll will continue to cop together the only difference is ya'll will be dealing with my people directly. They are already comfortable with Simon, so the transformation will be smooth. Basically, I want ya'll to continue to move like a Triumvirate," said Wayne.

His reasons for wanting them to rule together was an attempt to prevent any one person from becoming too strong. He wanted them to maintain the balance that had worked so well for them over the years.

"What the fuck is a Triumvirate?" asked Fame, confused about the meaning of the word. This nigga Wayne is always trying to chase a motherfucker to the dictionary, he thought to himself.

"That means, all three of us are the Boss," responded Simon.

"That's absolutely correct," Wayne replied gleefully. He wasn't surprised at all that Simon knew what he was talking about because they had spent many of days chilling together in his crib, discussing how Marcus Ceasor was apart of the Roman Empires most infamous Triumvirate early in his career, so he expected such a response from Simon, who he considered to be a true student of history.

"All of you will run the organization from the top just like I did but ya'll will do it together. Any major decisions will be decided by a vote between the three of you. When two agree on how a situation should be handled then it's a go. That's the only way ya'll will move forward unless all three agree on what ever topic is at hand. There wont be any solo shit. Is that clear?" Wayne asked sternly looking at each of them to make sure that he was understood. When it was clear that he was, he continued.

"Each one of you is a Boss. Real always recognizes real, and that's why other bosses will gravitate towards ya'll. As long as the team stays together, ya'll will be able to elevate the Constellation of Hustlers and Gangsters to a level far greater than anything Simon's Dad or I, could have ever imagined. But ya'll have to keep the relationship with each other tight. Tug of war only exist between wanna be's. There are never power struggles amongst true generals. God forbid if ya'll ever do experience such a rift, then someone will have to die. Ya'll know too much about each other to simply part ways. And what ya'll have will never function successfully with a family feud going on. Don't ever forget that," Wayne Givens said ending his speech and officially ending his career of crime.

That evening at Tavern on the Green ended on a high note, full of promise. And for the next couple of months everything played out exactly how Wayne had envisioned that they would. The organization had expanded its reach and the money was flowing in and being divided evenly.

The Triumvirate as Wayne called them, was living up to all expectations. The world had been handed to them on a silver platter and despite their new found wealth and influence, for the most part, they kept their heads straight and handled themselves well. Everything between the three was perfect, that is up until Dana Sierra came into the picture.

CPSIA information can be obtained at www.ICGtesting.com
Printed in the USA
BVOW03s0829160414

350803BV00002B/170/A